ADAM

By
Eve Langlais

(Cyborgs: More Than Machines, #6)

COPYRIGHT & DISCLAIMER

Copyright © February 2015, Eve Langlais
Cover Art by Amanda Kelsey © February 2015
Edited by Devin Govaere
Copy Edited by Amanda L. Pederick
Produced in Canada

Published by Eve Langlais
1606 Main Street, PO Box 151
Stittsville, Ontario, Canada, K2S1A3
http://www.EveLanglais.com

ISBN-13: 978-1508615651
ISBN-10: 1508615659

PROLOGUE

Bang!

The sharp, cracking sound startled the intern in the lab. As she stepped away from her microscope, she eyed the open door leading to the hall. It wasn't unusual to hear explosions in this wing, as students experimented, sometimes with disastrous results.

Bang! Bang!

The echoing pops approached.

Should she take cover?

The expected alarm that would have signaled a lockdown never rang. Was the popping sound she heard the freshmen playing with firecrackers again? Every year there were some clowns who thought getting people to dive for cover was hilarious. Until they got suspended.

Yells, indistinct yet comprised of several voices, interspersed the occasional crack. The commotion drew nearer. Biting her lip, she peeked around for a spot to hide. If it were campus security chasing down pranksters, she'd feel foolish, but if it weren't…

Better safe than sorry.

Decision made, she searched in earnest for something to shield her. However, the lab provided no adequate cover. Before she could think to simply duck behind a counter, a large shape filled the doorway.

Her shoulders relaxed upon seeing the familiar visage of unit CG311, the cyborg guard who patrolled this part of the campus. Ever since the university had contracted his services, campus violence, especially against women, dropped.

"Hey, CG, what's going on outside?"

His gaze tracked over to her. "You need to hide." While his expression never changed, his words expressed worry.

Emotion from a robot? How strange. "From what?" she asked.

"Hurry." No denying the panicked thread in his voice.

Before she could duck out of sight, soldiers sporting visored helmets and padded chest armor poured into the room.

Unlike the friendly guard, these newcomers did cause a tremble, especially since they all bore weapons. A smoky smell followed them, permeating the air. But thicker still was the menace emanating from them.

What's going on?

"Unit CG311, kneel with your hands over your head," barked a guy with military stripes sewn to his sleeve.

The cyborg did as told, lacing his fingers behind his head.

She couldn't help but frown. "What's going on?" she dared to ask.

"This is a military matter, ma'am," replied the soldier in charge. "Please evacuate the premises. Corporal Kelly, escort her out."

"But…" The protest she might have voiced died on her lips as they trained their guns on the kneeling cyborg. A defenseless man who did not question why. She craned to see, even as the soldier pulled her away.

She noted the resigned expression in his eyes. Saw the emotion. He didn't flinch when the order was given. She flinched enough for the both of them.

"Terminate him."

"No." She never knew if she said it aloud or screamed it in her head. All she knew was she would never forget the blood—*oh god the blood*—that spattered from the cyborg as a half-dozen weapons fired at close range.

At her sobs, the cold military official rebuked her. "Stop those tears. He was nothing but a machine. A defective fucking bot."

But robots shouldn't bleed.

For a long time, she relived in her nightmares the horror of seeing the cyber unit terminated without a trial, without mercy. A man gunned down, whose only crime was being made into something more than he was born as.

It proved a defining a moment in her life. It was the day the military declared war on all cyborgs and the killing ensued. So much killing.

It was the day she realized that sometimes evil lurked beneath the surface of even the most unsuspecting veneer. From that moment forward, she made it her life's mission to find a better way to deal with cyborgs. One that didn't involve the savagery and blood that forever stained the floor in the lab—and her soul.

CHAPTER ONE

She works too much.

Adam would know, given he'd watched the petite scientist for a few weeks now. But not for any perverted stalker reasons, although the fact she liked to nibble her lower lip was something he duly noted even if it bore no relevance to his mission.

Dr. Laura Cowen was intriguing for reasons beyond her cushioned buttocks, the lazy strands of hair escaping the messy bun atop her head, and the glasses she continuously pushed up on her pert human nose.

The curvy doctor was in charge of a very special project, one involving the highest level of security, where she and she alone had access to some very intriguing samples.

Samples Adam wanted to get his hands on but had yet to figure out how to acquire. The closest he'd managed was having himself assigned as a security detail to this lab.

Guard duty. Yay.

Not.

It was the epitome of boring, and he could do it while using less than one percent of his processing capability. The only excitement and danger he'd encountered so far in his duties revolved around the fact that he was a cyborg working undercover right beneath the military's nose.

In your face, bastards. Talk about sticking one to them.

But now wasn't the time to gloat over his awesomeness. He'd received a coded text message on his phone before he'd gone on duty that had his mind looping.

Things were about to get interesting.

Long time no talk. I'm coming to town and was thinking of popping in for a visit with a few friends. Think you can put us up for a few nights? Signed, *A.*

A as in Anastasia, his ex-girlfriend and the closest he'd ever come to a normal relationship. Or at least the human equivalent of one. Some things were hard for him to grasp, such as love and commitment to one person.

In his world, people, even cyborgs, served needs. In this case, Anastasia fulfilled a coital purpose. Pleasantly, he might add, and while he did miss having a partner he didn't have to hide from, he didn't mourn her loss like so many humans did when a partner moved on.

Not missing her though didn't mean her return didn't cause a blip of interest. Why was she back? And who did she bring with her? Last he'd heard, she was on a deep, undercover mission aboard a military vessel in space, determined to find those who'd made her into an enhanced cyber unit, and once she located them? They'd pay. Anastasia wasn't one to show mercy.

Nor was she one to pop in out of the blue. Something of import must have brought her back to Earth. But what?

Questions and more information as to her sudden reappearance required addressing. However, he dared do so only through secure channels. A top secret military operation buried a few levels deep wasn't the place to make inquiries, even if he could wirelessly tap into their network. Given that might compromise his cover, he refrained and kept his mind on his work.

Work? Ha, as if guarding the lovely doctor presented any kind of chore. On the contrary, imagining what the lovely doctor would look like with fewer layers of clothing helped pass the time, and pleasantly.

Exactly eight hours and three minutes after he began, his shift ended. His replacement—late as usual—arrived to guard the lab, and still the petite doctor worked.

She works too much for a human.

But what she did, or didn't, wasn't his problem. He had other affairs that merited his attention more than the working schedule of a human scientist.

Adam submitted to the different levels of security as he clocked out. Unlike some of the other soldiers, he opted to live off the premises, something the military had to allow given their barracks within the hidden installation had suffered an unfortunate fire that had taken most of the living quarters.

What a shame.

Rats in the wiring was the official verdict—unofficially, the rats were excellent carriers of tiny bombs that left nothing of their origin. Such a fortunate turn of events—for him. A lack of living space within the facility meant he could come and go instead of being forced to live under constant watch.

Exiting the last layer of security—which involved invasive pat downs of his body to ensure he didn't smuggle anything—he collected his cellphone, which had no new messages, along with his other gear, from his locker. Given he could regulate his body temperature, he didn't technically need the jacket.

However, given his human pretense, he wore it for the sake of appearances.

Exchanging polite pleasantries with other soldiers delayed his departure, but despite his urgent desire to leave, he maintained a normal appearance. Undercover work meant playing a role. In this case, he needed to fake being a human, and he did it to the best of his ability.

Why, he'd even say he was more human than many of the men he worked with. Less modest, though.

After some promises of gathering for a few beers later that week, and hey, they should get together and watch the game, he was striding through the dark parking lot to his car. A super boring Acura four door. All a common soldier could afford on his salary—with a few hidden modifications.

The metal body was lead-lined to block intrusive outside signals, but lest that rouse suspicions, it was also coated with a specially enhanced paint. The innovative clear coat sheath on his vehicle could create a pingback so scanners registered his body, and any other cyborg occupants, as human and also made sure detection units ignored the fact that he had a missile strapped against his muffler. A cyborg never knew when he'd have to blow some shit up.

His seeming stock radio, set to a popular country music channel, contained a powerful computer, which fed him information and gave him access to the Internet and cell signals.

As for the cooled interior of his armrest, did it refrigerate stolen samples or hold deadly viruses? Not quite. But he insisted on having it for his stash of Coca Cola and chocolate bars.

Even cyborgs had junk food vices.

Sliding into the driver's seat, Adam started his car and pretended to fiddle with the radio channels as he scanned for bugs, tracking devices, or bombs. Complacency was a cyborg's enemy.

It took him only a few minutes to return with a clean verdict. Satisfied, he drove to his lair, which he referred to as his cy-cave—just not out loud lest his cyborg allies mock him.

They would mock me because they're jealous. Like a certain superhero's, his cy-cave contained an array of supercomputers, wickedly cool gadgets, and a modified muscle car that, while lacking a rocket booster engine, could go from zero to sixty in less than two seconds.

If he were a plain human, he might have gotten a boner the first time he was pressed against the driver's seat with almost g-force. As he was more evolved than that, he allowed himself only a wide grin.

Where was this most amazing lair you might wonder? Under a mountain? In the city sewers? Carved out in the tunnels linking their subway transit system?

Unfortunately, he wasn't so fancy. Adam's super-secret hideout was in his basement. An expanded basement existing below the crawl space of his home, a small bungalow he rented from a corporation, which, under several umbrellas of identity, technically belonged to him.

The perk of being the rebel cyborg leader on Earth.

The revolution, which he first started in his basement apartment once he began his new life after escaping the military's clutches, had evolved since its inception, especially as he brought other cyborgs on board, or at least those he didn't smuggle off planet. He also allowed some humans sympathetic to their cause to help.

With their aid, he and the other survivors of the military extermination carved out their secret hideout and then, over time, furnished it until it now rivaled any command center the military owned.

Pulling into his driveway, Adam scanned his neighbors before exiting his vehicle. His heat sensors didn't detect anything out of the ordinary, unless the small squirrel perched in the tree was a spy.

Possible. Look what he and his kind had done with rats and robotic flies.

Much as Adam wanted to rush to his subterranean hideout, he held himself back. One never knew who might be watching. Who might be recording his movements and reporting them. When a person worked for the government and military, especially at his level, the layers of security proved many and varied.

Big brother spied. And big brother eliminated. It was up to him to stay ahead of the game and to fool them into thinking him the perfect human soldier.

Like any man coming off a long night shift, he shed clothes upon entering his home and turned on the television, a sports channel of course. He microwaved a barely palatable meal. Thank goodness he didn't rely on just that for nutrients. He'd starve for sure. No wonder so many humans were unhealthy.

He also cracked a beer, but that was more for his personal enjoyment. He turned off his metabolic processor for alcohol and allowed himself to feel the buzz that came from ingesting fermented barley and hops.

While he performed these mundane tasks, his BCI—short for brain computer interface—pinged his detection network, which comprised hidden cameras and microphones, not just in his home and yard but also spanned the length of his street at intervals. Clever spies always watched from a distance.

Nothing blipped his radar. All appeared in its place. He'd made it through another day. His cover appeared intact. Time to put his human persona to sleep.

Teeth brushed, peeing with the seat down, and stripping naked, he scratched—even though he didn't itch—on his way to bed. He crawled under the covers and feigned sleep.

He checked around him, casting out his wireless senses. All clear.

Flip time. Literally.

Under the guise of turning over in his sleep, Adam turned over in truth. His bed acted as a secret entrance—only one of many—that dropped him into a chute that led directly down to his command center.

Did he allow himself a tiny thrill as he slid down the ramp? Yes. One of his fractured memories was of him as a child doing the very same thing at a park, the exhilaration of flying down the plastic chute and then soaring as he hit the bottom was one of his purest remembered moments of actual joy, a joy from when he still retained his innocence.

His expression showed nothing of his inner glee as hit the floor with his two bare feet and stood without a stumble. As if his cybernetic reflexes couldn't handle such a simple maneuver.

Adam stepped into a pair of track pants he kept on a hook by the slide, not out of any sense of modesty—nothing to be ashamed of down there—but more out of respect for the humans he worked with who seemed more acutely aware of nudity.

Betcha Dr. Laura would blush to see me in the flesh. Although he'd rather see a blush on her face because of passion. Would she moan as he caressed her body or bite her lip to hold back any sound?

Months of practice allowed him to control an erection at the thought, but he really wished his tech team would find and correct the error in his programming that made the control necessary in the first place.

"I'm here," he announced.

"Duh," replied Rosalind, who never turned from her console.

"No respect," he muttered.

"Bite me," was her retort.

It made Adam grin. How he loved the feisty nature of the woman who acted as his eyes and ears when he was away. Rosalind had come a long way since he'd found her.

The petite, dark-skinned female was a cyborg he'd rescued from a human brothel, their trash disposal bin more specifically. When an overly enthusiastic client damaged one of her organic eyes and detached an arm—for what fetish, Adam never did ask when he held the bastard's throat, crushing it as the man's eyes bulged—they left Rosalind, previously known as Project R969, for dead.

Thanks to a tip, Adam arrived in time to save her.

Seeing her leg disappear into the maw of the garbage truck, with its deadly crushing gears, he'd sprinted to the rescue, knocking the attendant unconscious, stopping the teeth from churning, and lifting the broken body from the refuse.

The fleshly wounds healed quickly due to her

nanos, but the severe ones, like her eye and arm, took months to replace. Finding cybernetic limbs on the black market wasn't easy. After the great cyborg purge a few years back, all things mechanical, even for the benefit of humankind, came with a stigma. No one wanted to be accidentally considered a cyborg, lest the military, or vigilantes, come after them.

Foolish superstition. Cyborgs were more than cybernetic arms, legs, and eyes. Even an electronic heart didn't count. A true cyborg had not only a giant chip in its brain but also nanobots in their body. But apart from that, they were still human. They could bleed. They still retained fleshly tissue and organs, most of the time. In some cases, those were replaced with more efficient units. Just having a few mechanical parts didn't make someone a cyberunit. Only those governed by the alien tech were the true cyborgs.

And yes, he'd said alien. But that was a heated discussion for another time.

"About time you got here," Rosalind purred in her sex-kitten voice, which she knew grated on his nerves. Originally programmed for coital services, she retained some aspects from her previous life, the sultry voice being one of them. "You'll never believe who sent us a coded message."

"I already know. She texted me, too. But what I really want to know is what's up with the plaid pants? Didn't that fashion faux pas go out in the eighties?"

Rosalind continued to tap one-handed as she held up her other hand in a single finger salute. "Plaid never goes out of style."

"Says you. So any clue what she wants?" he asked as he took a stance behind her and scanned the screens. Nothing jumped out at him.

"Maybe she's come back to declare undying love."

He snorted. "Anastasia? Nothing comes between her and a mission." Not even a comfortable partnership in and out of the bedroom.

Okay, so he might have fibbed a little before. It did bother him that she'd left. She was the only woman he'd ever considered equal enough to call a girlfriend. Not because he lacked opportunity. His human lovers could never get enough, but Adam never hooked up with the same woman twice. Given his secrets, it was safer that way.

With Anastasia, though, he could be himself, not hide who he was. It proved refreshing. In the spirit of maintaining their coital status, he gave her the space she demanded and helped her advance her personal mission. And yet, despite all that, she'd walked away from him, and never looked back.

Until now.

"What does she want?" Had she tired of her mission in space? Had she missed him?

He'd thought her crazy to leave the comforts of Earth for the uncertainty of galactic travel. Not to mention, a cyborg living in a city with a population of a few million stood a better chance of blending than a beautiful woman surrounded by hundreds of men on a spaceship.

And that was where their argument started. They could not get their logic to follow the same pattern. Odd, given they both sported the same model BCI and level of programming. However, somewhere their variables didn't match up, probably because she lacked the awesomeness of a Y chromosome and a penis, but he never said that aloud. Anastasia would have probably ripped off his dick and slapped him with it otherwise.

Unlike some of my cyber brothers, I prefer a real cock to the rubberized and motorized version.

"She's on her way to Earth and needs help getting past the planetary defense system."

"Easy enough. Swing some aviation codes to her so she can land. We'll have to send someone to pick her up."

"She's not alone."

Something he'd conveniently forgotten, which, given his eidetic memory, was technically impossible. Just another flaw in his programming that would have to be dealt with. "Who's she with?"

Swiveling in her chair, Rosalind grinned. "Her husband, for one."

Unexpected. So, Anastasia wasn't returning to resume where they'd left off. A shame. But worse than the fact that she'd reconciled was the true dilemma. She was bringing her husband for a visit.

Adam grimaced. Just fucking great. If ever there was a man Adam wanted to stay far away from, it was Seth. If cyborgs had one fault—other than deciding they wanted to live on their terms and throwing off the shackles of their imprisonment—it was jealousy.

Perhaps they could blame the extra testosterone in their systems. Or the fact that now they could enjoy life again. Whatever the reason, when it came to certain possessions, and especially lovers, many of his kind were infected with an irrational need to protect.

Mine. A word that used to have no meaning to them while their minds were prisoner, but became all-consuming once they were liberated.

Want to bet Seth will have an issue I used to have coitus

with his wife?

Best to avoid the male altogether. No use antagonizing the super spy that Adam and others were modeled after. Stories of Seth's exploits peppered the underground cyborg news—circulation twenty-seven. Most chose to move off planet once rescued, unable to live a day-to-day existence that could end suddenly and violently if discovered.

"What are they doing here?"

"I don't know, but they're not alone. They've also got another one with them. Avion."

The mention of the name startled him. "He's alive?" Through the cyber network, he'd heard news of Avion's destruction during a raid on an asteroid that hid a military base.

"Alive, but sick from my understanding."

A frown creased his brow. "Sick? How is that possible? Did you misunderstand?" Not likely unless Rosalind's programming was buggy. Still though, cyborgs didn't fall ill. Their nanos fought all known infections. "Is it a computer virus?" Did he need to worry about his network? Should he install a pre-emptive security firewall?

"They didn't elaborate. However, I was given the impression his situation is terminal and one of the main reasons for their visit."

Terminal and from something other than a well-placed bullet? The very concept sobered him. "Is that all? Anyone else with them?"

"They've got a flight crew, commanded by Aramus, but he and the others aren't staying. Their mission is to drop off Anastasia, Seth, and Avion."

"For what purpose?"

"They didn't say."

Didn't say, but Adam would bet it was important if they were coming to him for aid instead of sneaking planet side on their own. "I want you to fabricate three identities."

"Connected or strangers?"

For a moment, Adam thought of telling Rosalind to make Seth and Anastasia fake siblings, but pettiness over the fact that she'd run back to her jerk of a husband was irrational, and beneath him. "Make them husband and wife, with Avion as the brother."

"On it. What about accommodations?"

"I want them here with me. Friends in town for a visit." Because anything that brought three of the rebelling galactic cyborgs to Earth must be dire, and as leader for the Ethical Treatment of Cyborgs—his public marketing title when he loaded videos to the internet—he needed to find out more about the issue with Avion and his supposed illness.

Because if the military has finally found a way to shut us down, then we need to know about it and find a cure.

CHAPTER TWO

The military guard with the intense blue eyes was back again. Not that she paid him much notice. Actually she tried very hard to pretend the six-foot-four, linebacker-wide, clean-cut soldier didn't stand sentinel. She didn't quite succeed.

Although they'd never technically spoken, and barely exchanged the briefest of glances or nods of acknowledgement, she couldn't help a certain fascination where he was concerned. Tish, her best friend, said it was lust because Laura hadn't gotten laid in ages—so long that there were probably cobwebs up her pie hole, or so her raunchy friend claimed. Whatever the cause, Laura couldn't deny her attraction to the man, but, oddly enough, there was more than just a primal lust that drew her.

He fascinated her. She wanted to study him—and not just naked. She was convinced there were secrets hidden beneath his stoic expression. Secrets she wanted to unravel.

And she was certain he wanted to explore her further, too—possibly naked.

Despite his position outside the lab door, she could have sworn he watched her. Crazy given he faced the opposite wall in the hall. Yet every time he pulled a shift while she worked, which was often given her workaholic tendencies, her skin crawled, not unpleasantly mind you, more a tingle of awareness that she didn't feel with any of the other soldiers.

Nuts. Perhaps Tish was right. Blame it on a lack of physical intimacy.

The body was a wondrous machine capable of making its needs known in the oddest fashion. This stalkerish fascination for the guard could be her subconscious talking to her. *I've gone much too long without indulging in some good old-fashioned skin-to-skin contact.*

In her defense, it wasn't entirely by choice. She worked long hours. Long hours in a regulated military lab, where most of her interaction was with other scientists—who, quite frankly, didn't even remotely come close to making her pulse rate flutter. She also ran into soldiers quite often. It was a military base after all, but they were under strict orders to not interfere with the scientists—or socialize with them.

Something Dr. Jenkins and that female private learned to their humiliation when the general called them out publicly on their shameful, licentious behavior.

"We are a strict no fraternization facility," he'd barked when he'd called a staff meeting. *"Which, for those who need to understand what I mean in plain English, means we don't fuck while on military property in broom closets or on lab counters."*

Dishonorable discharge and the loss of the research opportunity of a lifetime wasn't worth a few minutes of coital relief.

Hence, why she ignored blue eyes. Mostly.

Concentrating on the task at hand, she let her hands nimbly pull her latest specimen from the centrifuge, a machine that essentially spun sample ANMC018 and, in the process, helped separate it into different parts. Laura didn't know where the test liquid came from, other than it was hemoglobin based. Simple facts were denied her. Heck, the military wouldn't even tell her if it came from a human, if it was man-made or a genetic anomaly—although she had her suspicions.

Varied tests led her to believe the blood originated from an actual person, but it was the deeper analysis where things got weird.

The plasma and platelets, while sequencing into a proper DNA strand, held not one, not two, but five extra chromosome strands. Strands of a shape that no amount of searching could match.

Nothing earth-based she would have wagered.

Fascinating, yet, at the same time, frustrating, especially since Laura sensed she was on the verge of discovering something mind-blowing. Impossible some would even say. Because extra chromosomes wasn't the only strange thing about the sample. If her theory was correct, the tiny inert particles in the blood were microscopic bits of nanotechnology. Tech that, according to the military and media reports, should no longer exist. Tech she couldn't measure or gauge because all the samples she got were already dead.

Whatever the teeny tiny robots in the blood were meant to do, she couldn't say with certainty—but she could guess. Guessing, however, wasn't acceptable in her field. Science relied on cold, hard facts, not a hypothesis that the nanotechnology she worked with came from a cyborg.

Cyborgs no longer existed because they were all supposed to be killed on sight and incinerated lest they rise again. The extermination order was courtesy of their current government and enforced by all law personnel and the military. Even some more psychotic fringe groups got in on the killing, some overzealously so. Ever since the cyborg uprising, anyone with artificial limbs or parts was ostracized and in danger from the extremists who vowed to eradicate all cybernetic beings.

If this sample came from a cyber unit, then what did this mean? Was the military holding a live one for testing? Had they preserved a body? Or was this an attempt to somehow combat the cyborgs or reactivate the cyborg program?

All questions with no answers, a cruel jest for a mind that liked to know why. It frustrated her almost as much as the stubborn tech she could see through her microscope but had resisted all her attempts to reactivate thus far.

Even though it galled her, she'd practically begged her superior for more information. That didn't get her far.

"I need a fresh sample."

"You have what you need."

"Perhaps if I could see where it came from?"

"That's classified."

"Can't you give me even a clue as to what you expect me to achieve?"

"Figure it out."

Figure it out, they said, and so she worked blind. Without a basis of comparison, or even the slightest idea of what to expect, she tread in unknown waters, hoping for a lucky fluke, which shouldn't be how science worked, and yet some of the greatest innovations and cures, she reminded herself, were found by chance.

Or accident.

"Damn." She cursed as the vial she held slipped through her gloved hands and smashed on the floor. Despite knowing the protocol for such an incident, her first impulse was to drop to her knees to clean up the mess, even as a siren went off.

The female robotic voice announced her clumsy

shame to everyone. "*Contamination in Lab three. Evacuate the immediate premises and report to the outer chamber for decontamination.*"

Ah hell. Laura sighed. So much for her latest attempt to reactivate the nanos. It would have to wait. Dropping the chunk of glass she'd snagged on the floor, she stood and headed to the sealed and pressurized door leading to the detox chamber.

Stepping in, she tried not to flinch as the portal behind her slid shut and clicked. Locked in an eight-by-eight room, all glass so it wasn't entirely claustrophobic, she still didn't like the small space. She also didn't like the fact that Blue Eyes stood just on the other side of the exit, rifle held slung over his chest in a ready position, his eyes tracking her every move.

His orders? If she tried to avoid the decontamination or showed signs of illness, keep her there or, if she tried to escape, shoot her. The military might have reassured her that the sample she played with was benign, but at the same time, they weren't screwing around with it.

Placing her glasses on a shelf, Laura closed her eyes as the first layer of cleansing began. A rain shower of water from overhead, a chilly one, sluiced her from head to toe and siphoned through a floor drain. It was followed by a mist, some kind of cleansing agent, which supposedly killed any live bacteria on contact.

Next step, remove her gear. Given the samples she worked with weren't considered hazardous, she didn't have the goggles and air exchangers others had to wear, but she still had her hair bound in a plastic cap, her hands gloved in rubber, and wore a long lab coat, which was resistant to fluid, but not impermeable.

Her street clothes were slightly damp, and if she

were done for the day, she'd usually keep them on and step out at this point, but this was a decontamination procedure. As soon as she'd shed the coat and hair net, the shower came on again, soaking her.

Lovely. So much for the silk blouse that said dry-clean only.

The deluge of water stopped and left her dripping. She wasn't quite done.

"Please remove all your garments and place them in the disposal chute."

Strip to the skin? Surely he wouldn't make her? Her gaze met the soldier's, but his smooth expression didn't reveal anything.

"Must I?" she queried. "I didn't get any on the coat, so I doubt my clothes are a risk."

"Orders, ma'am."

The military and their damned orders.

Lips drawn in a tight line, she stripped from her soaked garments and dropped them into the chute that led to a sealed oven, which used extreme heat to disintegrate contaminated items. Standing in her bra and panties, she dared him to say something.

He did. The bastard. "All of your clothes, ma'am."

"Can you turn around?"

"Sorry, ma'am. My orders are to watch you for signs of infection."

Watch. More like leer, the pervert. And to think she'd entertained lusty thoughts about him. Not anymore. Inwardly grumbling, she shed her undergarments, and while she didn't meet his gaze, she was aware of it and couldn't help but blush.

Panties and bra tossed in the trash, she hugged herself and glared through a wet hank of hair at her guard. His face might not show emotion, but she couldn't help but note his gaze seemed more intent than usual. Despite her annoyance at his insistence on following the rules, she couldn't help the awareness flushing her skin. She also couldn't help an inappropriate mental question.

Does he like what he sees?

As a doctor, even one dedicated to molecular level science, Laura knew she didn't possess the ideal body proportion. Definitely not a model type. At best, she could be described as cute with her short and plump frame. Too much time in the lab and not enough on a treadmill. Her milky-white skin rarely got kissed by the sun, and fluorescent lighting did little to help her pallor.

Which meant the heat in her cheeks was probably flushing other parts of her. *I hope he thinks it's because of the decontamination and not because I know he's watching.* Because truth told, while embarrassment accounted for some of her pink coloring, arousal also played a part.

How sad that getting naked for a stranger turned her on.

Her gear disposed of, and her body rinsed again to clear it of contaminants, she snagged her clean glasses and jammed them on before she let the heated blowers air dry her, the warmth rather pleasant after the chill of the acrid, antiseptic spray.

Turning around in a three-sixty at the orders of the automated system, she inadvertently caught the gaze of the soldier. Caught it and held it.

While his face might have remained expressionless, his eyes told a different story. A woman knew when she was being admired, and despite her sporadic experiences with the opposite sex, Laura was no exception.

He likes what he sees.

A pity nothing could ever come of it.

The irritating computerized voice announced, *"Decontamination completed. Please proceed to your superior's office for debriefing."*

"Right after I find some clothes," Laura grumbled as she opened a sealed cabinet and pulled out a fresh lab coat. Wrapping it around her nude body hid it, while paper slippers covered her bare feet, but she remained all too aware of her lack of panties and everything else. Good thing she kept spare clothes in her locker. She'd learned her lesson after her first accident. Going home wearing only a lab coat and curly, haloed hair made the neighbors talk.

Eyes downcast, Laura stood before the door and waited for the soldier to release it. With a hiss of air as the sealed unit was breached, the portal slid open.

She stepped out.

"Please follow me, ma'am, for your debriefing," the blue-eyed soldier said, speaking to her for the first time, and oh my, while she might have joked with Tish that he probably had some high-pitched voice, something imperfect to ruin his allure, she was wrong. So terribly wrong.

His deep voice without the machine filter of the intercom hit her senses like the smoothest of chocolate. It rolled over her skin with a decadence that only made her crave more.

She couldn't hide a shiver. "Brr. Is it me or is it cold in here?" she said, trying to divert his attention. "I need some clothes. So if you don't mind, we need to hit the locker room area first."

"My orders are to take you directly for a

debriefing."

Attraction or not, Laura didn't bend to his command. Wouldn't. *No way am I going anywhere with my lower parts uncovered.* "Not until I change into some real clothes. I refuse to conduct a meeting while wearing only a lab coat." She met his eyes as she stated it, pulling on her years of dealing with men who thought they could bully a woman just because she chose science as a career instead of homemaking.

"No?" A hint of a smile curved the corner of his lip. "You do realize I could make you obey."

"Yes. I don't think there's any doubt you could. But I'm hoping you won't."

"If you must. Walk quickly. If we're going to detour, then you need to do so rapidly."

He took off at a brisk pace, and she scurried to catch his long stride.

"Thank you."

"Don't thank me yet. I'm risking a reaming by not following orders."

"But at least you're showing yourself to be human."

He stiffened at her side. "What's that supposed to mean?"

"Nothing. Just that I'm so used to you standing guard outside the lab, all emotionless and robot like. It's nice to see you have feelings." And a sexy voice to match the hot package. *God, I need a break.* More like sex. Her mind really was on a dirty roll today.

He laughed. "I am nothing like a robot. And I can assure you, I most definitely *feel.*"

Yes, he did feel, hard and strong, at least his fingers did as he kept a grip on her and propelled her down the hall at a fast march. Why the need to hold her she couldn't have said. She wasn't about to flee. Perhaps he did it so that it seemed he had the situation in control to those possibly watching from the many cameras mounted in the ceiling.

As they rounded the last corner before the locker area, he halted, jerking her to a stop. Turning a startled gaze his way, she said, "Why are we stopping?"

"You're bleeding," he stated.

"No, I'm not…" She trailed off and stared in consternation as he raised her hand. Angling her index finger, she noted the tiny pinprick of blood on the tip. She must have cut herself on the glass from the shattered vial.

Oh no. Her gaze darted to meet his, the impact of the tiny wound making her heart race.

She'd cut herself on the debris but missed it during the decontamination. Not good. The usual procedure in such a scenario was to keep her quarantined, watching and testing her for at least five days for even for the tiniest of possible infections.

I don't want to be put in lockdown. It sucked, mostly because she hated small spaces and she couldn't abide cable television. She'd much prefer to read or work in her lab, but those things would be denied her.

Such a tiny, tiny wound, yet the soldier's choice was clear. He had to report her.

Or not.

Holding her gaze, he lifted her finger tip to his mouth and dabbed it with his tongue. A shiver went through her, definitely not cold induced.

"Why did you do that?" she asked, her voice huskier than usual.

"Never heard of a kiss to make it better?"

"Embracing it with lips doesn't heal."

"And yet, you're more relaxed than you were a moment ago."

"I wouldn't be so sure of that. It's hard to be relaxed when you've got the prospect of getting locked in a cell for observation for almost a week." And she didn't doubt they would lock her up, even for a sample they'd reassured her was benign but still required the following of rules for contagion.

He arched a brow and smiled. "I won't tell if you won't tell."

Seriously? A brilliant smile illuminated her face. "Thank you."

"Don't thank me yet. You still have to get dressed and get moving if we're going to keep the director from handing us both our asses."

"I'll just be a minute. Thank you." On impulse, she stretched on tiptoe and placed a kiss on his cheek, an act no one could see because the smart soldier had halted them in between cameras to let her know of the blood.

Speaking of which, how had he known she bled? The cut was pinpricked sized. She'd not even felt it. He must have seen it somehow.

Keen gaze. Then again, she'd already sensed that about him, that he noted everything around him, down to the smallest detail.

Meeting her soldier in person, at last, brought her intrigue level up a notch. Great physique, handsome appearance, a fresh, clean scent—yes, she'd noticed as they walked down the hall—an observant personality, and a voice meant for decadent whispers.

He had to possess a flaw, and she was determined to find it, right after she found some underwear and got dressed.

CHAPTER THREE

Standing guard within the locker room, Adam did his best not to think of the pretty doctor stepping into underwear. Nor would he replay—again—the image of her removing them when forced to undergo decontamination.

It didn't take a brilliant mind like his to know it embarrassed her. Red cheeks, downcast gaze, elevated heart rate. Even if he didn't have orders to watch, he wasn't sure if he could have looked away.

When the alarm clanged, he'd whirled, not because of protocol but because his first impulse was to ensure the doctor wasn't unduly harmed. *Although why her well-being matters, I've yet to figure out.*

To his relief—an odd emotion he almost didn't recognize having not really encountered it before—she'd just had a clumsy moment, but that human lapse had led to some control-stressing moments as he was forced to watch her undergo the various levels of decontamination.

A proper gentleman would have looked past her. A true soldier would have leered. But Adam was a cyborg. He controlled his emotions and his acts. Cyber units always acted depending on what the most proper course was according to analysis of the situation.

Except in this situation, confronted with the nudity of a woman who fascinated him, he wasn't a machine, but a man. He stared, he noticed, he lusted, and he felt. Felt aroused mostly.

In that moment it didn't matter how many nude women he'd seen in his lifetime. There was something about watching Dr. Laura Cowen as she shyly stripped that hypnotized him, spun his mind into a loop that wouldn't allow him to look away or to remain dispassionate.

When she exited, wearing only the thin lab coat, he kept reminding himself that she was off limits. No touch. NO. TOUCH.

The command struggled against his base wants. He didn't let his primal instinct win.

Other than his grip on her arm, which was for any cameras watching, to make it seem like he was doing his job and the one in charge of their direction, he managed to stay focused, until he caught the hint of a wound.

I smell blood. In between watching cameras, he halted them and brought her finger to his mouth, lapping it, feeling the sizzle of connection at the simple touch, seeing her eyes widen, not in consternation over his act but a reciprocated sensual interest.

The lick served a dual purpose. First, the receptors in his tongue could perhaps taste a trace of what the vial held. What did the doctor work on? Had enough of it entered her bloodstream for him to find out?

That was the most logical reason for his action. The second was selfish. It gave him an excuse to touch her. Lips on her skin.

She'd not startled or drawn away. On the contrary, her lips parted, her gaze softened, and her core temperature rose.

She is attracted to me.

A heady revelation he desired strongly to act on.

As for when she kissed him quickly on the cheek? A good thing she left to dress out of sight in the woman's locker room.

Was it wrong for him to wish, instead of organic orbs, he had a more advanced pair of robotic ones that could have seen through the portal and played voyeur?

What was wrong with him? *Behave.* Or at least pretend to.

He was a soldier with a job to do. A cyborg with a mission. Apparently not a very bright one, given he'd foolishly told the woman he'd cover up the fact she'd hurt herself.

If he got caught, he might be subject to more than a reaming. What if he was reassigned? He'd lose his chance at finding out the secrets of this military facility.

A smarter cyborg would have done his job and kept to the mission, which would have meant ratting out the doctor. Adam, though, didn't always do things by the book. He liked to think of himself as more evolved and intelligent than the computer in his brain.

His human half helped him to process events differently than his BCI, hence his offer to keep quiet. A promise that served two purposes.

One. He wanted to gain her trust so he could perhaps foster a friendship and, in return, glean some information on the project she worked on. On the second hand, a tiny lick of the blood beading on her skin and he knew she didn't pose a danger.

Forget a science lab analyzing her blood and running tests, the taste buds on his tongue did in seconds what normally took hours. She was clean of any infectious diseases, so no use reporting her for nothing.

In this instance, breaking the rules—which always gave him a little thrill—would work in favor of his mission. Or so he told himself as he waited for her to exit, which she did quickly, having dressed in record time for a female.

Unlike other human women, the doctor eschewed makeup and complicated hairstyles. She'd simply bundled her damp hair with an elastic, forming a messy bob atop her head.

It charmed him. He could have groaned in frustration. How messy could seem sexy to such an organized being, he couldn't decipher. Nor could he stem the image of himself snapping the elastic and threading his fingers through her hair as it tumbled to frame her face.

Halt. Enough of this. Get your mind on the task.

As she approached, he gave a subtle sniff. He could tell by the lack of blood scent the tiny wound had sealed itself; no evidence to give them away.

"Ready to face the director?"

"Not really," she replied with a wrinkle of her nose.

Trailing behind her—a view he quite enjoyed— Adam escorted her to their superior's office, only a short distance away. Once there, he expected to be told to return to his post and keep an eye as the decontamination crew cleaned the affected area. To his surprise, the general stood at his receptionist's desk and addressed him.

"Stay, Corporal. I won't be long with the doctor. Once we're done, I want you to accompany her wherever she goes."

"Accompany me?" Laura frowned. "Since when do I need an escort everywhere I go?"

"Since our sources claim we've become a place of interest for a terrorist group."

"Terrorists? But we're a science lab. One that doesn't even test on animals. Not to mention we're supposed to be top secret. Why on earth would they target us?"

Casting Adam a look, the general gestured Laura to enter his office. "Come inside. We'll speak there." The implication? Where no one else could hear.

Adam could have smirked when the heavy door shut. As if his enhanced hearing wouldn't hear. Forget keeping secrets.

Standing at ease in front of the receptionist's desk, he tuned in his auditory receptors to hear what happened inside.

"So what's this nonsense about terrorists?" Dr. Laura asked.

"It's probably nothing, but given the price tag of the equipment and the top secret classification of our work here, we need to be careful."

Did anyone but him notice the general's concern was less about lives and more about material items?

"Careful of what exactly? What are we talking about? Staged protests? Graffiti? Vandalism?"

"I wouldn't worry if it were just that. Sources say the threat came from one of those cyborg-loving groups, their mandate something about the ethical treatment for cyborgs. Apparently, they are making noise about the facility overhead that houses us and have started rumors we're running tests on cybernetic organisms."

As the leader of the one and only true group for the ethical treatment of cyborgs, Adam knew the general's assumption was incorrect, but he did find the rumor interesting. He'd not seen or heard of any cyborgs being held here, but then again, he'd worked this post for less than a month. So far, his discreet forays on to the network hadn't netted him any indication of cyborgs on the premises, but peeling the layers took time. This place held many levels, virtually and physically.

"Cyborgs? Here?" Dr. Laura laughed. "That's ridiculous. They've been outlawed for years. They're so dangerous, the government has orders to terminate them on sight. No one would be crazy enough to think they could hold any prisoner."

It angered Adam to hear her thoughts on the matter. Somehow he'd hoped the doctor smart enough to see past the propaganda spread about his kind.

Yes, we kill, but only when necessary, and we do it in order to survive.

"I know, and yet there are some who believe we have some of the killers in custody. Utter foolishness."

Funny how the general agreed with her, and yet Adam's voice pattern analyzer detected his words as false. Noted and filed for a more in-depth look later.

"Now that you've been warned, let's move on from these silly rumors," the general said, changing the subject. "How is the research going? Any success in reanimating the samples we've given you?"

"No. I've run the samples I've received through several levels at this point. I've exposed them to different energy phases and levels. Attempting to jumpstart them, so to speak. Nothing yet has caused them to reactivate. Are we even sure they work?"

"They do."

"What kills them then?"

"That's—"

"Classified. So you keep saying. You're really making this harder than it should be," she said with a sigh.

Yeah, they were both making this hard. Adam wondered what they were talking about. What were they trying to reanimate? He got his clue a moment later and forgot to breathe—fake breath of course, given his body used the pores of his skin to absorb any oxygen he needed.

"Count yourself lucky you're even getting to see the nanotechnology."

"Lucky? I know what it appears to be, but I have only your word claiming it works."

"If you're requesting to see the source of the samples, then permission is still denied."

"Can you at least tell me if they're active from the source you're extracting from?"

"I cannot answer that question."

Could the general hear the doctor grind her teeth? "What a surprise."

"Exactly what do you think seeing the nanos active would achieve?"

"Seeing them at work might give me a better understanding of how they function. But more importantly, I'd like to see how they're shutting down. If I could see what triggers their, for lack of a better term, death, then I might be able to devise a method to reanimate them or stop it from happening in the first place."

The sound of fingers drumming wood was a telltale sign the general mulled over her request. His words confirmed it. "I'll see what I can do. But keep in mind, everything about the sample is classified, classified beyond what you're currently allowed to know as an outside civilian brought in for your expertise. To allow you access would mean a mountain of paperwork and even more stringent security."

"Good thing I don't have a life outside of work then," she said with a laugh.

And she wasn't kidding. Adam's background check on her had proved short and simple. Other than coming to work, she did nothing, not even go to the store. She had her groceries delivered, when she remembered she needed some. Her only real social time involved her meeting a friend every other Sunday for brunch. Same time. Same place. Same breakfast.

The doctor kept to a very mundane routine— one without a boyfriend.

It didn't surprise him when she left the general's office that, given the all clear to return to her lab, she chose to return to work. With Adam escorting her, silent given the traffic in the halls as the shifts changed, she went back to her scrubbed space.

Just before she entered, she placed her hand on his arm and shot him a smile as she mouthed, "thank you". He could have thought of better things for her mouth to do, but they required privacy.

As if the incident never happened, she returned to her research and he to his post standing guard until his shift ended.

Then it was off to the airfield to greet an old friend.

CHAPTER FOUR

Aboard a vessel just outside of Earth's orbit...

Relying on his other senses sucked. Big time. Avion wasn't used to inactivity. Once upon a revolution, he'd been a combat pilot, a soldier, a cyborg meant for action.

Not any more.

Now he was a cyborg dying.

No one came right out and said it, but he knew. His brethren lied as they mouthed meaningless optimistic words of encouragement. They shouldn't have bothered. Avion knew better. His nanotechnology, what made all of his various parts run, were dead, and without them to keep things regulated, Avion was slowly fading too.

A man more prone to emotion might have despaired and taken his life.

But even though the chances of his recovery were slim—odds calculated at less than five percent— Avion hung on and hoped, probably one of the most human things he had left.

He let hope guide his steps as he embarked on what he suspected was his final mission, a mission back to Earth. Clues they'd gleaned led them to believe the source of their origin was hidden there. Einstein theorized that, while a transfusion of their blood wasn't enough to jumpstart his nanos, perhaps if they could locate the origin of the tech, then maybe, just maybe, he could still be saved.

Avion harbored doubts about that. And even if the theory was correct, the clock was ticking down fast to the time he would suffer a complete shutdown.

One odd, yet intriguing, side effect of his loss of nanos were the dreams. Flashbacks in many cases of the life he'd once lived. As a man, not a machine.

He cherished those bright glimpses into his past.

But he obsessed over something he could have sworn happened only in his mind. Not long ago, during one of his sleep times—a real sleep, not one programmed or a shut down of his system for a reboot—he'd dreamed of someone. Actually, calling it a dream wasn't quite accurate. An alien consciousness had touched his own.

Who are you? he'd asked.

Her reply proved more puzzling than her mind-to-mind communication. *I am known as One.*

One of what? *Where are you?*

Hidden. A prisoner. One without hope.

There's always hope. Funny words from a man who hung on to only the thinnest tendril.

Not for me.

The sadness in her admission made his failing heart stutter and almost stop. *Don't give up. I'll —*

The contact abruptly shattered.

Find you. But she never heard his final words. And he didn't know what to think of his short conversation with the woman because his impression, even if the touch seemed foreign, tasted distinctly female.

Odder, Avion could almost swear she'd left a trace of herself behind. He didn't mention it to the others. They'd think him crazy. And perhaps he was.

The military had certainly done their best while he was in their custody to break him and had succeeded with his body.

But they'll never get my soul. That was if cyborgs even had a soul. Those against their existence vehemently argued they didn't. They forgot that all cyber units had started out as human as them.

Born human and, raised with freedom, until the military got their hands on Avion and the others. Their captors subjected them to treatments and operations. The military made them better. Or, as the military initially spun it to the media, enhanced their abilities. Cyborgs were created to be smarter, stronger, and all around more interesting.

Speaking of more interesting, the commotion on board their disguised ship rose a few levels as they entered Earth's orbit. They were about to find out if their contact from the surface rebel forces was a true ally or not.

Aramus, commander of the spaceship, had followed instructions to the tee. By masking their true ship name, the *SSBiteMe,* became something more mundane, *Star Dancer Shuttle Service.* Even though blinded, Avion could practically picture Aramus' grimace whenever someone said the name. He even had a logo: *Your shuttle to the stars.*

The grinding of Aramus' teeth was especially amusing when Seth told him he should change it to the *Shuttle of Love* and make it into a honeymoon ship. Good thing Aramus' human lover was on hand to stop the irritable cyborg from starting a brawl. Their fragile, on-board equipment couldn't handle a few tons of angry male flesh rollicking around.

Making his way to the command center, slowly,

the only pace he could manage nowadays, Avion eavesdropped on Seth, who had lost his habitual cool and good humor. A rarity, but then again, Seth wasn't used to dealing with jealousy.

"I still don't see why we need to meet up with your ex-boyfriend. We could simply land and go about our task on our own."

Seth's wife, Anastasia, sighed before saying, "And I've told you, numerous times at this point, despite your determination to wipe facts from your databanks, that Adam can get us in to classified places and give us access to information that won't require us wasting time."

"Because he's the overachieving head of the Earth-side cyborg resistance movement. I know. He's Mr. Altruistic."

"Not really. He's a murderous, cold, calculating cyborg."

"Not cool. I thought I was the most awesome murderous cyborg you know?" Seth didn't have to pretend affront at the comparison. He was genuinely insulted.

"Don't be jealous. You didn't let me finish. He, however, isn't half as entertaining, and definitely not as sexy as you."

Avion didn't need to hear Aramus' disgusted, "Get a fucking room, you perverted sex droids," to know they kissed.

Easing his way along the back wall, Avion slid into an empty seat. He didn't arrive unnoticed.

"Hey, Avion," Seth hailed. "You're just in time to find out if we're going to get blown into galactic chunks."

"Seth!"

"What, dearest wife? I'm just saying it's possible. I mean, you did, after all, dump this guy. How do we know he doesn't harbor a grudge? After all, you are so freaking awesome, what male could possibly handle your loss?"

Anastasia snorted. "You are such an idiot."

"I agree, but would both of you shut up before I get a blow torch and weld your lips fucking shut?" Aramus growled. "I'm trying to concentrate."

Avion smiled. Their BCI was more than capable of multitasking. Aramus grumbled for the sake of grumbling.

How Avion would have liked to tap into the wireless network and watch the proceedings as their ship performed the various checks and handshakes that proved they had permission to enter Earth air space and land. Not happening. Avion was unable to do even the most simple of cyborg things. He missed the constant hum of noise in his mind as his BCI absorbed information from everything around him and the mind-to-mind conversations that made him feel part of something. While many might not appreciate the hive-mind comparison, Avion missed the ability to share thoughts with his brethren.

"So far so good," Aramus mumbled, probably for his benefit since everyone else could see and *hear* with their wireless senses. "Entering the Earth's atmosphere in three, two, one."

Only the slightest of tremors vibrated the ship as they broke through the almost skin-like ring of pressure around their home planet.

For a moment, none of them spoke. While Avion sucked in lungfuls of air—damned human system required oxygenated breaths—the others forgot to breathe, all their focus attuned elsewhere.

"I don't detect any incoming missiles or threats," Kyle announced.

"A scan of surface communication frequencies shows no unusual messaging or indication that anyone thinks we are anything other than what we appear," Aphelion added.

"Goddamn it. Maybe Seth's partially right. Maybe this Adam fellow still has a thing for you, Anastasia. He's certainly paved the way for our arrival."

"I'm really tempted to ram your head through a screen," Seth groused.

Aramus chuckled. "I am so glad I volunteered for this mission. I've been waiting a long time to find something to rattle your cage."

"If we had time, I'd rattle you," Seth promised.

"Promises, promises. Guess you'll have to make it back alive if you want to wipe the gym floor with me."

"You aren't getting rid of me that easily, best friend."

A grumble of discontent rumbled from Aramus. "How many times have I told you not to call me that?"

"Sorry. I forgot we're secret BFFs."

Someone snickered.

"I'd gladly give that role to someone else. Say like your wife's ex, whom you're about to meet within the hour."

"I can't wait," Seth growled, the smack of a fist hitting his palm.

Neither could Avion, not because he would enjoy the fireworks between the males but more because something told Avion that the mystery voice in his head was somewhere on Earth—an illogical assumption, given a lack of evidence. Nevertheless,

Avion couldn't deny he suffered from some sort of gut instinct syndrome. Or indigestion.

Damned humanity. How he longed to be a true cyborg again.

CHAPTER FIVE

Going straight from work to the spaceport, Adam spared only a few minutes to change out his uniform—just as any normal human would do—before speeding to his destination.

Some folk were under the mistaken impression that abiding by the posted legal limits and performing proper stops and lane changes ensured a person flew under the radar. Untrue.

Those who adhered most stringently to the laws brought the most attention of all. Normal folk always skirted the edges of the rules. It was human nature.

Parking crookedly, his rear tire over the marked line, and shoving his card in to the short-term parking meter to buy himself an hour of overpriced space, Adam arrived—late.

Or, as he liked to call it, perfectly in keeping with his public identity.

As it turned out, his timing was impeccable. He spotted his trio of arriving friends and the space customs duty guard—one of his human recruits—giving them a cursory check over, the machine to detect for cyborg components temporarily bypassed to give them a green light of approval

Adam leaned against a pillar by the luggage carousel and waited for them, a nonchalant pose that belied his true actions. He scanned everything around him, from the couple toting the crying baby to the elderly couple who walked so slowly he almost offered to grab them and jog them to their departure gate.

As his guests approached, he straightened and offered a smile to his ex-girlfriend, Anastasia, who looked as yummy as ever even with her hair dyed blonde and cut short. She returned a smile of equal brilliance, which had the man by her side frowning. Hello, the husband.

Then, because he must suffer from a terminal self-destruct wish, Adam drew her into a hug.

"Adam," she laughed as he squeezed her, tight enough to crack human ribs.

Releasing her, with perhaps a hint of a smug smirk, Adam didn't even have time to blink before he hit the ground. For a moment, he saw gears whirring before he blinked and his eyesight returned to normal. *Nice shot, if a cheap one.*

"Seth!" Anastasia chastised with just one word.

The word did nothing for his jaw, which Adam had to unobtrusively pop back into place before anyone noticed its lopsided nature.

"Sorry. My arm just suddenly shot out. Some kind of glitch it seems. I'll have to run a diagnostic later."

"Glitch, my ass," she mumbled, but Adam couldn't help but note, as he sprang to his feet, that she didn't seem perturbed at all that her spouse might harbor a few loose screws. As a matter of face, her lips curved in clear, smug pleasure. *The brat is enjoying her husband's jealousy.*

And Adam couldn't help but enjoy antagonizing it. "Not his fault, Ana darling. He is, after all, one of the early models. He can't help but show his age."

To his surprise, because by his quickly run calculations his barb should have netted a violent result,

Seth laughed.

"I wouldn't underestimate my skills. Those who do, die, whippersnapper." With a smile that promised a violent battle—something fun to look forward to—Seth turned his back on Adam and called forth another man who walked slowly, cane tapping, eyes hidden by wide, wrap-around dark glasses.

This shambling ruin didn't require an introduction. It could only be Avion, but not the man Adam recalled seeing in some of the media vids where he was caught on camera, causing destruction—in other words, freeing cyborgs and confiscating goods. Adam couldn't help his uttered, "What the fuck happened to you?"

A rueful smile curling his lips, Avion didn't take offense. "I was a military guest for a while. The food was atrocious."

No joking. Signs of starvation marked the damaged cyborg. Never had Adam seen one of his kind so gaunt. Fragile.

It proved disturbing. One of the things their nanos did was absorb nutrients from their environment. It allowed them to survive substandard conditions with little need for resupply. A modern version of live off the land, an attribute Adam took for granted judging by Avion's appearance.

"Looks like more than a shitty diet to me. What really happened to you?" he asked. He didn't fear spies in this public place, not with all the noise and the fact he emitted a static hum that masked their words.

"This is what happens when you shut the nanos off."

"Off? What do you mean off? I've never heard of that happening."

"No one has. And yet here I am, living proof."

"I don't know about the living part. I'm thinking Avion might be the first cyborg zombie. Except instead of brains, he's going to start craving batteries," Seth teased, but Adam could see the worry in the man's eyes.

"If I need batteries, I'll go for your wife's night stand first."

"Hey." Despite the implication Anastasia kept power tools in her nightstand for satisfaction, Seth only pretended offence.

Anastasia shook her head at them. "This isn't funny, you two. Especially since what happened to Avion wasn't an accident."

"Someone has found a way to disable our nanos?" Adam asked. Until now, it was believed the only way to kill the bots in their bodies was to withdraw them from their body. For some reason, as soon as the nanos exited their host, they died. But in Avion's case, the bots within his body were dead. Talk about disturbing.

Seth snagged some luggage on the carousel, tossing the bulkiest bag at Adam—who, of course, caught it two-handed to keep up his human façade.

"They've managed to turn them off and we've not been able to do anything to reverse it," she replied as she looped her arm in Avion's. "We'll tell you all about it, but not here. Where's your car?"

"Right outside. It's the boring blue one."

Only once they were all stowed in the car and safely on their way—in other words, with no one seeming to follow them—did they resume their conversation.

"So spill it. What happened to you, Avion?"

"I told you they turned my nanos off, among

other things."

"Who did?"

Anastasia snorted. "Oh please. Has humanity rubbed off on you? Use your head for more than a rack for a hat. Who else but some military-owned scientists."

"Humanity is not a disease."

"Not according to Aramus," Seth snickered. "Although he's not as hardcore about eradicating them from the universe since he met his lady friend."

"He fell for a human?" Adam asked in surprise. While not completely unheard of, those most abused and least in touch with their past tended to harbor an intense hatred for the race they blamed for creating them.

"Fell and fell hard. For a while, he thought there was something wrong with his programming. He even had some of his friends knock him around a few times in the hopes of dislodging the problem. Alas, his affection for the human doctor was incurable."

"But less deadly than Avion's problem," Anastasia added, steering the conversation back on track.

"I still can't believe they turned his nanos off. Is it reversible?" Because of all the threats Adam faced, the slow, wasting death consuming Avion horrified him most.

"That's what we're hoping to find out. According to sources, there's a factory here on Earth, one dealing in special technology. Technology that might be based on the same platform as our nanos and cybernetic enhancements."

"You mean like that strange radar-cloaking device I've heard their warships are using?"

"Yes. But the invisible shielding from sensors

isn't the only thing you've got to watch for. Someone has also designed tracking bugs that are virtually undetectable."

Given Adam's constant need for secrecy and evasion, any technology that could out him was of interest to him. "What kind of tests has it evaded?" More and more, Adam drew lines between the clues, a picture emerging that gave even more credence to the theory that the cloaking technology and the nanotech the cyborgs bore were linked.

"The new bugs don't show up on ultra sounds, MRIs, metal detectors, or even x-ray. Heck, cyborgs can't even feel them."

"What do you mean?" Part of their internal diagnostics program included an ability to detect foreign objects in their bodies.

Seth replied. "As in I've held one in the palm of my hand and not known it sat there, even as I stared at it."

The conversation proved interesting, but not so much that Adam forgot to keep an eye out for someone following them. As he drove, he kept a constant watch on all his mirrors and kept a scan running on the police scanner and other frequencies used by the military and other agencies. So far they seemed in the clear. He did all this while, at the same time, asking pertinent questions of his guests. "If these bugs are so undetectable, then how are you finding them?"

"By accident initially. Once we knew about them, we began searching, but it hasn't been easy. Our saving grace is they emit the faintest of energy signals. While we can't actually feel their physical presence when coming into contact with the bug with our skin, the object can't hide the space it consumes. Physical exams where we manually palpate the flesh will reveal them."

"Is this your way of telling me you want to touch me all over?" Adam shot Anastasia a suggestive leer. Yeah, he baited a certain passenger, but this time he was ready for the fist aimed at the back of his head.

"Oops. Muscle spasm," said Seth, a tad too jovially from the back seat.

"You really should look at getting some of your parts replaced, old man." Despite the fact only the barest handful of years separated them, the barb made the spy cyborg stiffen.

Seth narrowed his eyes. "Anytime you want to test my joints…"

Anastasia verbally stepped between them. "I'll be testing them later, but in the meantime, can we get back to our mission? That is why we're here, is it not?"

Adam, seated in front of her, met Seth's gaze in his rearview mirror. He rolled his eyes as he mouthed to Seth, "Later. I'll wipe the floor with you."

A snort was the acceptance to the challenge.

"I know you're planning to get in a pissing contest," Anastasia growled. "I can see your reflection, Adam. Now is not the time."

"Spoilsport," he grumbled.

"I'm sorry. Let's just put Avion's dire needs aside so you and my husband can indulge in a pissing contest."

"I daresay Avion wouldn't mind if we took a few minutes to display our urinary prowess. I do have to go," Seth replied.

"Hamster bladder." The comment from Avion had them all laughing.

Adam caught Seth's grin and couldn't help one of his own.

"Fine. I'll hold it. For now. But only until the mission is done, my dear wife," Seth added, dropping a light kiss on her lips. "Because you are right."

"He finally admits it," was her dry retort.

Seth continued as if she hadn't interrupted. "Avion needs help, and fast. Our best lead at this point seems to involve going after the cloaking tech, which analysis says has a strong probability of having originated from the same technology that created our own nanos. In-depth research has led us to the one place on Earth that makes the cloaking devices. A factory outside the city owned by the military. It's said that while the highly guarded upper floors of the company are aboveboard, producing and assembling electronic devices for use by the troops, there is a secret lab below the factory, which is where the more out-there testing is happening."

Adam, who knew very well the factory he spoke of, dug for more information before revealing his close association to their target. "Out-there testing as in?" Adam prompted, preferring to get fact-based answers instead of relying on inaccurate supposition.

As he'd learned over the years, first from cataloguing human interaction and even with some of his more personal experiences, not all organisms, or even BCIs, came to the same conclusion given the same facts. It seemed personality and other outside factors could come into play.

"We believe they are creating a new weapon to use against cyborgs. Case in point, friend Avion. We also believe they haven't given up on their quest to enhance humans. Some of the things we saw in a secret laboratory hidden on an asteroid leads us to believe they're not just testing on cyborgs but humans as well."

"Tell them about the aliens," Anastasia murmured.

"Aliens?" Adam couldn't help the query. He'd only recently come to the conclusion that the military might be dabbling in science that wasn't earth-based in origin. What had his brethren discovered that made them sound so certain?

Seth shot his wife a look, to which she didn't reply but arched a brow. Seth sighed. "Testing has not been conclusive as of yet. However, things we discovered have led us to believe that our origin might not be Earth based."

"You mean we've got green Martian genes spliced into us?" Adam teased, treating the revelation lightly, lest he reveal too much. It was one thing to believe in an alien intervention, another to admit it aloud.

"Possibly Martian. Or Venusian or Plutonian."

"You forgot Uranus." Seth snickered.

She ignored her husband's juvenile rejoinder. "The point is, we're dealing with something completely unknown."

"Which is so reassuring," Avion interjected, finally joining the conversation.

"It won't be unknown for long. Obviously the military, or this factory, has access to samples that allow manipulation and splicing with the human genome. We need those samples. Perhaps they'll give us the answer to restarting Avion's nanos, or perhaps we can find a way to transfuse the nanobots without them dying."

Despite what the media and ill-informed human public thought, nanotechnology wasn't contagious. Yes, their blood carried millions of the little bots. However, as soon as the blood left their body, within minutes, all the nanos died. No one knew why. Some theorized they required life to animate them, but if that was the case, then why didn't re-injection reactive them? Nothing brought back even the slightest blip from the tiny suckers once they died.

Given their information, much of it new and some of it reinforcing his own hypothesis, Adam deemed it time to reveal some of his secrets. "This factory with the secret lab, I don't suppose it's called CyberGlys Technology?"

"Have you been eyeballing the joint too?" she asked.

"More than eyeballing. You're looking at one of the guards assigned to the lower level. But I'll tell you more about my scintillating occupation later. We're home."

Exiting his parked car, Adam took a moment to enjoy Seth's incredulous look.

"You live here?"

"Yup."

"But-but, it's suburbia," Seth sputtered.

"Yup. White picket fence and all," Adam agreed, unable to hide his grin as he led them to the front door.

Anastasia having seen his home before—as well as his bedroom—didn't gawk as she ushered Avion inside, but Seth couldn't help examining the mundane life he'd created for himself.

"Dude, this place is"—the spy model turned in a three-sixty, taking in the living room with its matching black leather recliners, chrome glass table covered in remotes, magazines, and even a classic empty pizza box, and finally stopped turning, eyes riveted on the huge plasma screen bolted the wall—"awesome!"

Pride made him puff his chest, an odd

mannerism he'd fallen into the habit of. Adam could claim it was acting. However, in truth, the human ego he'd cultivated came to him much too naturally. "Thanks."

"Is that an Xbox One and a PS4?" Seth asked in almost reverent awe as he snagged a remote.

"Yup. I've got the latest *Call of Duty*, too, if you're into shooter type games."

"Am I ever."

"Um, boys, I hate to break this super bonding, bromance moment, but don't we have more important things than video games to discuss?"

He and Seth shared a look that said it all. Women! Never letting them have any fun.

"You guys must be tired after your flight," Adam said aloud for the benefit of any possible bugs he might have missed, which, after their conversation in the car, now posed a worry. "Let me show you to the guest rooms."

In short order, Adam had them supposedly abed, their sleeping units modified like his in that they did a body flip and sent the occupants careening down the chute, leaving behind an inflated lump under the sheets meant to represent them. It wouldn't fool any but the most cursory looks, but it was better than nothing.

Conducting one final check that didn't raise any mental red flags, Adam arrived last, popping out the bottom of the slide and landing on his feet. It was only as he saw Seth hauling Avion from his sprawl on the floor that he belatedly thought of the broken cyborg's status. "Shit. I didn't even think to warn you about the ride."

The blinded cyborg managed a rueful smile. "Not your fault. Even I'm having trouble remembering this body doesn't work the way it used to. No harm done."

No harm, but given his fragile state, it could have hurt. Adam would have to keep that in mind.

Moving from the arrival chamber, they entered Rosalind's domain, where screens flickered, flashing data and images too fast for the human eye but just right for cyborg ones.

Nothing jumped out.

"I see you found our guests." Rosalind ignored her computer keyboard and swiveled in her seat to greet them. Only to find herself crushed in a hug as Anastasia smothered her.

"So nice to see you again," Anastasia enthused.

"Apparently. Good thing I don't need to breathe," Rosalind managed to say once she extricated herself.

Seth frowned at his wife. "You knew Adam had another female unit? Why didn't you tell me? You know Joe and the others have been looking for them."

Shrugging, Anastasia moved aside and leaned against a console. "Completely slipped my mind. I guess once we get out of here, we should let the others know."

"Ya think? Chloe's been pestering Joe about doing more to find her cyborg sisters."

"You mean there are more than just me and Ana?" Rosalind asked.

Seth, for once not leering or joking, took Rosalind's hand in his. "Yes. We've managed to rescue three so far, four if you count my wife. Do any of these names sound familiar? Chloe, formerly C791, her blood sister, Bonnie, once B785, and F814, Fiona."

"I remember them, especially Bonnie. I thought

she was dead. Last I heard the military had her slated for termination."

"We were all supposed to be terminated," Anastasia reminded. "Lucky for us, greed kept some of us alive, and cunning saved the rest."

"Speaking of cunning and saving, now that we're all gathered, I think it's time we discussed what you're doing here and what you hope to accomplish." Taking control early on, Adam hoped to circumvent any jostling for position. Perhaps it wasn't the most altruistic thing of him, and not in keeping with the cyborg hive mind, but he'd damned well built this resistance movement from the basement up, and he wasn't about to hand over the reins to anyone.

"Our primary objective is to see if we can find a cure for Avion. If the military has found a way to disable our nanotech and render us impotent, then it is imperative we discover out how they're doing it, devise a way to stop it, and figure out how to reverse it."

Funny how none of them raised the question of keeping the nanos inactive. Becoming human again would in some respects make their lives easier. They could live in the open. Resume mundane human lives. Problem was, once you'd lived with almost superhero powers, the idea of returning to something less was unfathomable.

"And the second objective?"

"Either steal the blueprints for the cloaking technology or destroy the factory creating it. If we can't adapt it for our own use, then we need to make damned sure the military can't use it either."

"Aramus is going to be extremely pissed if there are explosions involved and he doesn't get a chance to play," Avion remarked.

"When isn't Aramus pissed?"

"Good point."

"Our third objective is to glean any information about our possible origins. Any files we can scan, any rumors, pretty much anything at all relating to our creation is welcome. The more we know about how we were made, the better we can handle anything the military throws at us."

"And maybe we could reproduce and increase our numbers," Adam added, all too aware of the lives lost since the revolution started.

His statement startled his guests.

"Are you suggesting little cyborg babies?" Seth ogled him. "Dude. That is a seriously whacked-out idea."

"Is it? What race doesn't want to see its species continue? Why should we be any different?"

Anastasia, who'd not heard him expound this before, shook her head. "I thought the males had their sperm sterilized to prevent it from happening. I know the women have had their ovaries removed."

"Advances in science can replace just about any organ," Adam reminded.

A seriously discomfited Anastasia veered them back. "This isn't the time to debate procreation for our kind. We have our three objectives. We need to concentrate on those."

"Make that four." Avion, leaning against a wall listening, startled them all.

"Four? What do you mean four?" Seth frowned at the blind man. "Did I miss something during the briefing? If I did, I blame my wife. She's very distracting."

"Says the guy who was trying to feel me up

during it. But I'm with Seth on this one. I don't remember a fourth objective."

"That's because I didn't want to say anything before now. We need to add rescue to the list. We have someone we need to save."

As they exchanged glances, Adam realized no one knew what Avion was talking about. "Who? A captive cyborg?"

The wounded male shrugged. "I don't know who she is other than she spoke to me while on our way here."

"Spoke? How is that possible? I don't recall us getting any transmissions."

"She spoke in my mind."

As a cacophony of questions ensued, Adam held up his hand for silence. "Rewind, Avion, and help us out here. When you say she spoke to you, do you mean mind to mind?"

"Yes."

"But I thought your wireless capabilities were incapacitated when you lost your nanos?"

"They were, and still are, yet she still managed to speak to me. She called herself One. We didn't talk long, but from what I gleaned, I believe she's a prisoner and, given the fact that she could communicate with me, an important one to us all."

"And you're just telling us now?" Anastasia accused, hands planted on her hips in a very human gesture Adam doubted she consciously noted.

"I wasn't sure you'd believe me. I wasn't even sure I believed it myself. But since we've arrived planet side, it's almost like I can sense her."

"What do you mean by sense?"

"I guess the most apt comparison is a magnetic

pull. I feel drawn to a certain direction. I don't know how to better explain, other than I believe she is the one pulling me."

"Dude, if I hadn't been with you the entire trip, I'd think you smoked some seriously hallucinogenic drugs."

"Or he's suffering delusions brought on by his body shutting down because of the dead bots," Anastasia mused aloud.

"Or," Adam interjected, coming to Avion's rescue, "his condition has made him susceptible to contact with someone important to our cause. Whatever the case, if we're ready to believe in aliens, then we shouldn't discount what he says. So we have four objectives and, by the sounds of it, most center around CyberGlys Technology."

"Where apparently you work as a soldier," Seth added.

"I do, and it wasn't easy I'll tell you. I've been boot licking and yes sirring for the last two years now. I'm a corporal on guard rotation for a science lab under the factory."

"I'm sure I speak for all of us when I say, how the fuck did you manage that? I thought the military had screening in place to weed out cyborgs."

Adam smiled. "I'm just that good."

Rosalind snorted. "He means I'm that good. All screening protocols rely on computer programs. With the right hack, you can get scanners to ignore certain things, say like the metal in a certain dumbass' body when he goes through security."

"Why can't we implement that for every cyborg?"

"Because one re-route attached to a single ID is

easy to slide by, but when you start adding in more…" Rosalind trailed off.

"Gotcha," Seth replied. "So, we've got an inside set of eyes and ears. And?"

"And there is definitely something going on below the main factory. Something to do with the nanos. I just don't know what yet. My current mission has been to find out more, which, I'll admit, hasn't been easy. That place has got some hard-core security in place. But I'll let my expert tell you more about that."

Rosalind took over as they entered into her world of expertise—observation. "We've been watching this installation for some time. On the surface, it's a military protected manufacturer. They make toys, cool ones that aren't available to the public, although I'm sure they've sold a few on the side to those with deep pockets. But what those toys are has been unclear until your arrival. I'll admit, my sources didn't know about the cloaking tech or bugs."

"Not even rumors?" Seth couldn't hide his surprise.

Rosalind shook her head. "They are definitely keeping tight-lipped, and we've had little success discovering anything. Our biggest issue is their security is tight. Real tight. We tried to get a cyborg onto their production floor a few months ago. It didn't go so well."

A sobering reminder that, in their quest for liberation, sometimes casualties occurred.

Poor Simon, the guy who'd volunteered for the assignment. The special filter Rosalind added to him, a direct copy, or so they'd thought, of Adam's, didn't fool the scanning machine CyberGlys ran everyone through before entering their premises.

Before Simon could fake a breath, walls shot up around him, and the next thing anybody knew, he was gone. Vanished without a trace.

The same fate had yet to befall Adam, even though he worked on the even more secure lower levels. What made his programming different? How did he manage to bypass the scanners? None of his team could figure it out. But they kept trying to replicate it.

While a discussion arose about possible points of entry and weaknesses in the CyberGlys network, Adam's mind split off and pursued another line of thought. Just how far would he go to help his off-planet brethren?

While Adam trusted Anastasia enough to bring her to his secret cy-cave, he wouldn't blow his cover until he could be one hundred percent assured it would serve the cyborg cause—and could actually cure Avion.

The demise of one did not outweigh the greater needs of the many.

Adam knew once they acted and went after the secrets in the lab and factory level, they had to succeed the first time. There would be no second chances. Past experience had shown the military would close shop, wipe the place clean, and disappear, taking their knowledge with them.

Adam said none of this aloud, and he kept his mental receptors shut tight. While some cyber units enjoyed the wireless ability to speak mind to mind, Adam preferred to keep a cerebral silence. A strong sense of personal identity, as well as a fear of becoming a drone in a hive mind, made him someone who preferred to communicate orally.

"Seth and I will want to go over all the information you've gathered on CyberGlys. Maybe we'll spot something we can use."

"I'm sure we can find a workaround to this detection system they've got," Seth added.

Implication, *I'm smarter than you, and I will prove it by getting in.*

Challenged again. Damn, but if he'd known how much fun butting heads with an ex-girlfriend's husband could be, Adam would have done it sooner.

After months of tedious groundwork and patience, things were livening up. About time.

This revolution needed to get busy.

CHAPTER SIX

Are you there?

The mental query woke Avion from his slumber. For a moment, disorientation gripped him. Blinded, he couldn't immediately tell where he was. His fingers groped and felt the cotton of sheets.

He didn't have to stretch far to locate the mattress edges. A narrow bed. He sniffed. The faint aroma of dust. No noise or hum of machinery. Recollection returned as his sluggish mind put the pieces together.

I am in Adam's house. The spare room to be exact. The spot he'd returned to after their meeting. He was abed, where he caught some real sleep, something his broken body needed too much of these days.

But forget his location. The whispery touch against his thoughts came again.

Did I imagine you? Have I finally lost my mind?

He sent back a message, thinking it, not saying it, and really hoping it wasn't he losing his own marbles. *I'm here. Is this…One?*

You're there! He couldn't mistake the happiness in her exclamation. *I wondered if you truly existed.*

I'm real—if doubting his sanity. *Where are you? Can I see you?* Okay, maybe not see given his blindness, but at least meet in person.

I am a prisoner. There are no visitation rights for me. Unless we count those in the suits with their needles. That is the only reason why I can contact you. The shielding has been

64

temporarily lifted as they've returned to collect more samples.

Samples of what?

Me. My blood. My essence.

Why?

Because I am One.

An enigmatic answer if Avion had ever heard one. But he wasted time. Who knew how long this contact would last? He needed to ask the more pertinent questions. *How is it that you can talk to me?*

Your mind isn't as noisy as the others'. They cannot hear my voice over the cacophony of their tasks. But you, your mind does not have the same taint. You shine like a beacon in the darkness when they open the door.

Door? What door? Are you locked somewhere?

Locked. Buried. Forgotten. I am the One, and they keep me hidden.

Who? Who keeps you hidden?

They leave now, and the doorway will be shut.

When will it open again?

An hour, tomorrow, perhaps never. Find me—

The communication abruptly ended, the lingering plea unfinished yet all the more poignant because of it.

More than ever, Avion was determined to do something to save the woman. The woman who called herself One. A woman he suspected was within reach.

This time their communication had been much stronger. Closer.

Even if it weren't, it wouldn't change his determination. She needed him.

And while he didn't like to rely on something so imprecise as gut instinct, he couldn't deny the almost omen-like certainty that he needed her even more.

CHAPTER SEVEN

Arriving at her lab, Laura was surprised to see her supervisor, hazmat garbed and leaning against her research table, waiting for her, a small, unmarked cooler by his side.

"I'm sorry. I didn't realize we had a meeting," she said once she entered, which took a few minutes as she gloved, robed, and masked herself in her protective gear.

"We weren't scheduled to meet. However, I have a surprise for you. I took your request to a higher-up last night."

Which request was he talking about? She'd made a few as she recalled. She couldn't help glancing at the cooler. Had at least one of them come true? She let nothing of her optimism show in her face.

"And?" she prodded.

"And I've brought you a new sample. A live one."

Her heart just about stopped. "You mean, the nanos work in it?"

He nodded. "For now, but they won't remain alert without a host for more than a few hours. So test the hell out of them while you can. I can't guarantee when or if I can get you another batch."

"Then why are we wasting time talking? I need to get to work."

She didn't spare her boss a glance as he exited into the decontamination chamber.

A live sample. What she'd hoped for ever since she got her first glimpse of the nanos.

Rushing to and fro, she launched a series of tests. The vial of blood, a bright red, a vibrant splash of color on her slides. The droplets she dropped into various tubes turned a variety of colors as she added elements to them, playing with the samples, in a rush to record as much data as possible.

She cursed when a drop escaped a pipette and hit the metal countertop. What a waste, but useless for testing now, given she couldn't know if it was contaminated. Ignoring the miniscule spill, she got another drop and plopped it onto a glass slide. Viewing it under the microscope, she orated aloud her findings, knowing the audio system in the room recorded everything she said.

The tiny bots didn't emit any kind of energy signature that her devices could read. If it weren't for the fact she could see them moving and multiplying in the sample she viewed, she'd have never known they were there, or active.

But more important, what could they do? Since she wasn't given live subjects to work with, not even a beady-eyed rat, she had to test using other substances.

Ebola virus introduced? It never even got a chance to start its destruction before the bots swarmed and destroyed it.

Cancer cells? Gone in seconds.

Every vile thing she introduced was wiped in but a moment. A blink of an eye in some cases.

Amazing. What this could mean for society…

She truly wished she had something more interesting to test on or to compare to. Gut instinct told her she dealt with the same nanos that powered the cyborgs and their enhancements. Was the reason the bots died because the samples lacked a BCI to keep them active? Or was it the organism itself that kept them powered?

So many questions, and time ran low. Already the bots showed signs of slowing down, some of them sluggish on the last injected sample.

The drop on the table mocked her. Stared at her. Dared her.

But cameras watched.

As she swapped slides, she nicked her glove, out of sight, the tiny tear small enough to escape scrutiny. She could barely breathe and expected to hear sirens blazing at any moment as she pretended to swipe a rag across the single spot. In truth, she passed her finger over it, the slight rip smearing the sample on her skin, not much and probably for naught.

The chances of the minute particles surviving the decontamination chamber after she peeled off her handwear were miniscule, and yet she did it anyway.

Thumbed her nose at the rules. Defied the military.

Some things shouldn't be kept a secret.

Some things deserved to be exposed.

Sometimes chances needed to be taken.

During her frazzled back and forth testing, the guards had changed. Blue Eyes was back on duty, and she tried to focus on him and their encounter the day before instead of the criminal act she'd just performed.

I wonder what his name is. Hopefully something manly like Chase or Travis.

He would certainly manhandle her if he suspected what she'd done. The soldiers had their orders, and they followed them. Yet, hadn't this one given her leeway yesterday?

But one minor incident didn't mean she could trust.

Frustrated when her fresh sample became just as inert as all the others, she decided to call it a day.

Entering the decontamination chamber, she did her best to shield the tiny section of finger with which she dabbed the blood. It didn't work. Once she'd stripped her gloves and lab coat and disposed of them, she could see no trace of red on her digit.

Great. She'd taken a chance and failed.

Still, was it any wonder when the intercom blared to life she jumped, certain she was about to get called out?

"Dr. Cowen, please report to the director's office, and would the corporal on duty please accompany her?"

Caught?

Maybe she worried about nothing. Maybe it was just the director wanting an immediate report on her findings with the live sample.

Exiting the decontamination chamber, wearing clothes this time, she met the gaze of her guard and offered a shy, "Hello."

"Hi. Done early today?"

Apparently he'd noticed her workaholic tendencies. Then again, her ridiculous hours were hard to ignore. "I wasn't getting anywhere, so I thought perhaps I'd indulge in a good night's sleep."

"Sleep is overrated," was his murmured reply.

It took her aback. *Did he just flirt with me?* Unsure, she didn't reply.

He strode alongside her toward the main offices. "What's the director want?" he asked.

She shrugged. "Who knows? Probably a status report." *Or to call me out and have me arrested.*

But as it turned out, she was wrong on all accounts.

Master Sergeant Philips met them in the outer office. "Doctor, thank you for coming and sorry for calling you in here. However, due to certain security threats, which we've had to upgrade from mild to serious, it's been ordered that none of our researchers be allowed to exit the premises or travel unescorted."

"Why?"

"A fringe group has threatened to bomb the installation. Probably a hoax that won't amount to anything. However, we don't wish to take any chances. Corporal, your orders are to escort the doctor to her home. Inspect the premises for anything suspicious and remain on duty, out of sight, until you are relieved at twenty-two hundred hours."

"You can't be serious," she exclaimed. "Surely this group you speak of won't be waiting for me at my condo."

"We can't be sure of anything at this point."

"That's just crazy. I don't want a soldier on guard outside my door. I have neighbors. What will they think?"

"Then keep him inside. The fact remains that we are taking every precaution to protect key team members. Refusal to comply means we will be forced to find you accommodations here in the facility."

Given the regular quarters were still under construction, that didn't leave any pleasant options. "So either locked up here or under watch at home? Nice choices." She couldn't resist the sarcasm.

"Which will it be, Doctor?"

As if there was a choice. "Home."

A lower lip sulk proved impossible to fight as she left the office and grabbed her things at the security checkpoint before exiting the facility. Despite the assurance that her escort was for protection, she couldn't help feeling as if her rights were being ignored.

Heightened security at the installation she could understand, but to have someone shadowing her? Expecting her to have the military invade the privacy of her home? She didn't like it one bit.

Invite him inside indeed. Although, the thought of having her handsome guard in her home did rouse more than just anger. Home meant no prying cameras. A bed. Privacy.

Apparently her body viewed events differently. *But there will be no hanky-panky.* At least none initiated by her.

If he were to make a move though…

She veered her mind away from that naughty direction.

It was obviously fanciful thinking. Blue Eyes hadn't said a word during the entire exchange with his superior other than to say, "Yes, Master Sergeant," when asked if his orders were clear.

A good-looking guy like him wouldn't jeopardize his career for sex with an overworked, under-exercised science geek.

Before she could mentally list all her faults, she employed her self-empowering speech. *I am a beautiful, strong woman. I don't need a man's attention to know I'm special.*

But she sure could use a man to remind her what it felt like to be a desirable woman.

Sigh. She hated it when she argued with herself.

Leaving the building, the evening air bit her

cheeks with its chill. She shivered as she tucked her chin down into the collar of her coat.

"Cold?"

"A little. Aren't you?"

Dressed in only his uniform with no jacket, Blue Eyes didn't seem affected by the lower temperature at all.

"I'm tough. I'll survive," he replied with a grin. "Which way to your car?"

She pointed as she strode in the direction. He remained close to her side, hand on his holster—his rifle having been handed in before they left the building—ready to shoot. Despite her disbelief that anyone would want to harm her, apparently her guard took the threat seriously if the way his eyes scanned the lit parking lot was any indication.

It gave her an urge to shout "Boo!" just to see how he'd react. Petty, but then again, she wasn't feeling too generous. After her failure to smuggle a sample, and then paired with a babysitter, not to mention her struggle to resist her guard's allure, she was in no mood to be charitable. Especially once he snagged her car keys from her hand just as she aimed them to unlock her Mazda3.

"What are you doing? Give those back."

"I'll be driving." Firmly said.

His imperious decree helped fight against her attraction to him and fed her ire. "Says who? It's my car."

"But I've got orders and evasive maneuver training."

"Since when does the military have their soldiers practice driving?"

"They don't. But I've played enough video

games and watched enough movies to know how to spot and lose a tail."

Mouth agape, she stared at him. Speechless.

He laughed, a rich sound that should have irritated her, especially paired with his takeover of her vehicle. Instead, warmth swirled in her lower body. The jerk was much too handsome. And while she doubted his supposed evasion skills, truth was, he probably drove better than her. Just ask the half-dozen scrapes and dings on her car.

Distracted driving was what her last ticket said. Not her fault her mind wandered. Commuting was boring. Why couldn't scientists hurry up and build an automated car?

Before he slid into the driver seat, he circled her car, even dropped to a knee to peer under it.

"What are you doing?" Other than presenting a delightful view of his butt as his combat pants stretched taut over it.

"Checking for bombs."

A long blink helped her process his words. "Bombs?"

"Yes. But lucky you, your car seems clear."

"Yay for me," she muttered as she got into the passenger seat and buckled up.

Sliding into the driver seat, he grimaced at the tight fit. He fumbled underneath for the lever to push the seat back. He fiddled with all her presets, from her mirrors to her steering tilt.

The situation irked more and more. Laura wasn't used to people in her space, and he wasn't just in her space. He was changing it.

As he reversed, he must have caught something in her expression because he asked, "What's wrong,

Doc?"

"What could be possibly wrong with having a virtual stranger driving my car and being ordered to babysit me?"

"I don't know if I'd call us strangers. I've been guarding you for a while now."

"And yet yesterday is the first time we ever actually spoke."

"True. But not because I haven't wanted to. You're usually working when I go off duty. Besides, how can you not feel a certain connection to me now? I did, after all, see you naked."

He might have meant the comment and grin as a teaser, but it just made her blush.

"Please don't remind me. I'm not in the habit of stripping in front of men whose name I don't know."

"Adam."

"I'm sorry, what?"

"I said my name is Adam. So now we're not strangers anymore."

"A name is supposed to make us friends?" She wrinkled her nose at his logic.

"Hmm, I suppose since you're a doctor, you need a few more facts. I get that. Here goes. I am twenty-eight years old, a Sagittarius. I like watching and playing football, kicking butt in video games. Live on pizza. Hate brussel sprouts and sing in the shower."

"You do not."

"What? Sing in the shower?"

"No, live on pizza." Her lips curled in a smile. "You're too fit for that diet to work at your age."

"Are you calling me old?"

"No, merely pointing out that an established metabolism for your body type requires more nutrients than simple dough, cheese, and sauce could give."

"Well, I do pile it with protein and veggies too."

Laughter bubbled forth as she rolled her eyes. "Oh, that makes all the differen—Eek!" She couldn't help a yell of surprise as he swerved her car, cutting across a lane of traffic and darting down a side street. "What the hell!"

"I thought someone might be tailing us," he replied, not glancing at her. His eyes were trained on the rearview mirror.

She couldn't help but crane to peer behind them. "Did you lose them? Are we being followed?"

"They didn't follow. False alarm."

Suspicious, she stared at him. "Did you seriously think someone followed, or were you just doing that for fun?"

"Would I do something like that?" So innocently said.

"I think you would."

"See, you know me so well already. I told you we weren't strangers. So, Doc, now that I've spilled my guts, what's your story? Or is this going to be a one-sided friendship?"

Given his attempt to make things between them easier, and her genuine enjoyment in his flirtatious demeanor, she couldn't resist his charm. "My name is Laura. I am twenty-nine years old, a Scorpio. I like to read. Work. And I also live on pizza."

The admission had him swerving again. "Bullshit. Um. That is, I mean no way."

"Why not?"

"Well, you're a doctor. Aren't your type all about the healthy eating?"

A roll of her eyes and a snort let him know what

she thought about his assumption. "Have you seen the hours I work? I tend to forget to do groceries, and when I do actually buy some, I forget to eat them. I've thrown out numerous science experiments dug out from an abused fridge. Enough that I no longer keep much in it. Since delivery is my friend, and my hours are whacky, my choices usually involve hitting a fast food drive-thru, ordering in pizza or Chinese. Pizza usually wins because I can eat it cold on the way in to work if I don't have time to grab breakfast."

"So does this mean I shouldn't expect you to put on pearls and heels and cook me a nice meal when we get to your place?"

"I don't wear heels because they hurt my feet." And the last time she twisted an ankle. "The only pearls I've ever had were the bath kind that melt, and as for me cooking? Only if you have a death wish."

His boisterous laughter filled her car. "Fair enough. We'll order in."

Ice broken, they chatted about their favorite restaurants around the city. They finished the drive without further incident. As she guided him into the underground parking garage situated beneath her condo complex, his jovial manner migrated to serious, as, once again, he scrutinized the darkness and the shadowy space between parked vehicles.

"What's up with the lack of lighting?" he asked.

"We've had problems lately with vagrants sneaking in and smashing the bulbs. Management keeps saying they'll do something about it, but they haven't yet. Something about the budget and needing enough votes from the residents."

"It's a safety issue. How can a matter like that even be up for debate?"

"Nowadays, every decision, even the most basic ones, seems to require a committee. Lucky for me, my spot isn't far from the elevators."

Exiting the car, she hadn't taken a step when Adam loomed by her side. He gripped her upper arm and strode quickly to the elevator.

"What's the rush?"

"We're not alone," he muttered in a low breath.

The words sent a chill down her spine, and she tucked in closer to him. Surely no one would think to accost them. He was friggin' soldier. One carrying a sidearm, which remained holstered at his side in spite of his belief they might have company.

Before she could ask him why he didn't have it in hand, from behind a fat concrete pillar, a trio of thugs stepped. Heads shaved, pants slouched low and bunched over combat boots, they appeared a motley bunch.

Unlike her armed escort, they had their weapons out. A switchblade, a metal rod, and a small pistol. A triple ouch.

"Hand over your purse and wallet, and we'll be on our way," the ringleader said, smacking the metal bar against his empty palm, a meaty-sounding threat that brought forth a tremble. She fumbled the strap to her purse off her shoulder, ready to comply.

With muggers, it was sometimes just easier to give in to their wishes. Her purse and its contents could be replaced. Broken bones would take longer to heal, and scars would last forever.

However, apparently her companion didn't share the same philosophy. "I don't think so," Adam replied.

Big surprise, the answer didn't go over well.

"A hero?" sneered the one with the gun. The muzzle angled upward until it leveled out at face height. "Let's see how brave you are when you're eating a bullet, army dude."

Laura froze, fright paralyzing her limbs.

Not so Adam. He moved so that he stood in front of her, his body a barrier between her and the menace. As a gesture, it was nice, but in practicality, he was neither knife-, bullet- or skull-smashing-rod-proof. "I'm going to give you the best advice you're ever going to get. Leave now, or I will make you hurt." Inflammatory words to a gang obviously used to getting their way.

"What are you doing?" she whispered. "Just give him your stuff."

"Why would I do that?" An incredulous note tinged his words. "These miscreants don't frighten me. They chose the wrong person to accost."

With that overly confident statement, the situation erupted.

And it was Adam who started it.

One second, he stood before Laura, a human shield. A blink of her eyes later, and he'd twisted into action. Not one to watch adventure movies, or even sports, Laura couldn't help but gasp, and wince, as Adam displayed his military training.

Surely it wasn't natural for a leg to rotate so high and for a foot to connect so solidly? The impact of Adam's boot to the guy's jaw knocked the one toting the gun to the cement floor, the weapon flying from his hand and skittering off into the shadows.

In a blur of motion, which had a fascinating grace even given the violence, Adam managed to duck the swing of the heavy metal rod, which surely saved him from a crushed skull whilst, at the same time, lunging with one hand and grasping the wrist of the knife wielder.

The timing was impeccable. Impossible she would have said, and yet she watched it with her own eyes.

Adam must have applied intense pressure to the wrist he'd snatched because, with a cry of pain, the guy let the blade clatter to the ground. It proved a less ominous sound than the crack that preceded the shrill shriek of the knife man. Hugging his arm to his chest, that attacker staggered away from Adam. Turning on a heel, he fled, leaving only one conscious thug.

The remaining mugger loomed larger than the other pair, and he showed no sign of backing off. Lips pulled back in a sneer, he taunted Adam, displaying a valid reason for the war against drugs because surely only a mind frazzled by abuse could think at this point he had even a slim chance of winning. "You'll pay for that. I'm going to mess up that pretty-boy face of yours until even your mama doesn't recognize you."

"You can try, but it's not going to happen. As a matter of fact, I'll guarantee, by the time we're done here, you'll wish you'd stayed home and watched re-runs."

The fist Adam threw practically blurred, but the impact was visible. With a thud of flesh hitting flesh, it connected, and blood gushed from the mugger's split lip.

With a bellow of rage, the guy retaliated. The metal rod swung, wildly, the air swooshing with each pass. Adam danced on his feet, keeping just out of reach. But he didn't keep quiet.

"Missed me." *Whoosh.* "Missed me again."

Whistle. "Come on, can you put a little effort into it?" The wild swings continued to fail as Adam taunted his assailant.

A motion from the corner of her eye caught Laura's attention, and she turned her head to see the gunman shaking off his dizziness. More worrisome, while the fight distracted them, he'd managed to retrieve his weapon and aimed it with a wavering hand.

She yelled his name in warning. "Adam!"

Several things happened at once.

With uncanny speed, Adam knocked her to the side, sending her into a parked car and jostling her glasses loose. As she turned around, even with her blurry vision, she could see Adam dash towards the gunman, propelling the big mugger ahead of him.

"Stop or I'll shoot!" the gunman threatened.

Adam didn't stop. Instead, he hoisted the guy with the rod and tossed him just as the gun fired. Airborne, the big guy flew into the pistol holder, and they both went down in a heap of flailing limbs, but only for a second before Adam hauled the pair up with astonishing strength. Gripping them by their necks, he knocked their heads together before dropping them again, unconscious.

Silence ensued as Laura blinked and tried to make sense of the insanity, which, at most, probably lasted only a few minutes.

What to say. What to do. She truly didn't know how a person should act in a situation like this.

The same paralysis didn't affect Adam. He bent down to grab the mugger's gun and tucked it in his waistband. "We shouldn't leave this lying around," he said as she gaped at him. "I wouldn't want any kids to get their hands on it. Are you all right? You didn't get injured in the scuffle?"

His concern for her was sweet, but she wasn't the one who'd thrown herself in harm's way. "I'm fine. The question is, are you all right?" she asked. At such close range, she found it hard to believe the shot fired had missed. Vision fuzzy without her lenses, she squinted but couldn't discern any damage.

"Fine. Just fine. Nothing a little bandage won't fix. Where are your glasses?"

Good question. As she stepped back so she could peer at her feet, she heard a crunch. "I think I found them."

"I don't think they're gonna work so well anymore," he said with a rueful smile as he crouched to pick up the lopsided frames with a missing lens.

Given this happened to her more than she liked to admit, she always kept spares. "I've got another pair in my condo."

"What do you say we get out of here then and go find them?"

"But what about those guys?" She gestured to the muggers, out cold on the floor. "Shouldn't we call the police or something?"

"And spend the next few hours at a precinct answering questions? Gee, that sounds like fun." He grimaced. "Let's not forget that involving the cops means you'll then have to go back a few more times to answer more questions, maybe even attend a trial. For what? So they can give these fellows a year or less for attempted robbery? Do you really want to waste your evening doing that?"

When he put it that way… "But shouldn't we do something to get them off the street?"

"Let's be honest here. Given our justice system,

these guys will be back out on the street within twenty-four hours, forty-eight tops. Until someone takes care of them permanently, or they kill someone, I'm afraid society is going to have to put up with them."

"That seems rather harsh," she said with a frown as he ushered her into the elevator. Her hand shook as she inserted her access card into the slot. He placed his steady hand over hers and helped her. The doors dinged as they shut, and the elevator lurched into motion.

"I'm surprised you have such sympathy for dregs of society who wouldn't have thought twice about hurting us, and for what? A few dollars, maybe a credit card?"

"So your solution would be to kill them. Without mercy or a trial."

"Yes. What would you do?"

"Give them a chance to redeem themselves. To show them another way, a way that doesn't involve violence and give them a chance to change their lives."

He snorted. "An optimistic view. Let me ask you though, what would you do if they don't change? What then? Incarcerate them for life? Make the taxpayers foot the bill? Let them loose to continually reoffend and escalate their crimes."

"I don't know. Maybe this makes me a softie, but I think that even the most maligned deserve a second chance."

"Monsters should be killed." He didn't wait for her reply as the elevator door opened and he stepped out.

Given the seriousness of the discussion and their disparity in agreement, she kept silent. In this case, he was probably right. Those thugs weren't the type to easily change their path in life. But she couldn't help remembering another time, and another man, a man who died without trial or a chance for redemption.

Adam stopped without being told before her door. With her nerves more under control, she slid her access card into the slot the first time. With a click, the lock disengaged, but she wasn't allowed to enter.

Inserting himself between her and the door, Adam murmured. "I need to go in first and check for company. Since the hall seems clear, stay here. Only come inside if you see someone coming. Otherwise wait for my all clear."

All clear for what? Ah yes, the supposed threat. In a sense, she should count herself lucky he'd been with her tonight. While the muggers in the parking garage weren't terrorists, they could have full well done her a lot of harm had she arrived alone. Single women didn't fare well against gangs. She might have lost more than just a purse tonight if not for his intervention.

It took only moments before he gave the signal. "Your place looks clean. You can come in now."

Clean? He'd obviously not peeked under her furniture where dust bunny families thrived. With not a small amount of sarcasm, she said, "Thanks for inviting me into my own home."

An unrepentant grin graced his lips. "Sassy. I like it."

And with his flirtatious words, her irritation disappeared—in regards to him at least. Adam didn't give the orders that forced him on protective detail, just like he couldn't help his beliefs that criminals deserved just punishment.

In a sense she believed the same thing. Crime should have penalties, but what about those forced to go against the laws? What about those whose only fault was their very existence, an existence not wanted by society?

In case it took pointing out, she wasn't talking about children of ghettos or broken homes. When she thought of those unwanted and persecuted simply for existing, she meant the cyborgs.

Laura never forgot that day years ago in the lab when soldiers shot the unarmed man.

But his wasn't the only death that haunted her. She couldn't un-see the video footage of the culling of cyborg ranks, a pirated video that went viral on the Internet showing the military slaughter of dozens of frozen soldiers whose only crime was the chip in their brain, a chip the military had installed.

"Hunh?" It seemed while she woolgathered, Adam asked a question.

"I said, is there any other access to your condo other than this door?"

"The balcony, but given we're about eight stories above ground, I doubt we can expect company via there."

"You never know. Grappling hooks and rappelling gear are easy to order."

"You really should work on your reassurance speeches," she muttered as she peeled off her coat and boots.

"I deal in reality, Doc, and that means facing the truth whether we like it or not."

"Well, at this moment, I'd rather worry less about facing the truth and more about getting into something comfortable."

Too late she realized how that sounded.

"I like the sound of that." As he eyed her head

to toe, his gaze lingering in between, her cheeks heated. It wasn't the only part of her warming up.

"Um, if you'll excuse me, I'll be back in a bit, and we can order in some food."

He headed her off before she made it to her bedroom. "I need to check in here first."

As he prowled her space with its unmade bed, clothes scattered on the floor, and general disorder, she felt a need to explain. "I've been kind of busy lately and have let the place get kind of messy."

Turning to face her, Adam grinned and his blue eyes shone. "I'll admit this is fascinating. The fastidious doctor in the lab is a slob."

"I'm not a slob," she protested even as she grabbed at a pair of glasses lying on top of her dresser, which boasted empty panty hose packages, two antiperspirants, and, damn it, was that mold growing in that coffee cup?

He arched a brow.

Her nose wrinkled. "Okay, maybe I'm a little messy."

His smile widened.

"Okay a lot. But don't tell me you're Mr. Clean. Or are you? If you're going to hang around here for a few hours, feel free to tidy up." Hopefully wearing fewer layers. Starting with him stripping off that long-sleeve shirt and—

Mashing her glasses on her nose brought her world back into sharp focus. It also enabled her to clearly see the man before her. "Is that blood on your sleeve?" Noting the dark patch on his arm, she reached out to touch it, only to have him angle away.

"Just that tiny scratch I mentioned. Nothing to worry about. I don't feel a thing."

She frowned. "You really should clean that."

"I will as soon as I check the rest of your place." Pivoting on his heel, he popped into her bathroom for a moment, checked her closet—a brave task given things sometimes had a tendency of falling out in an avalanche—then, with a grin, Adam left her room, shutting the door behind him.

Alone. And yet not.

As Laura stripped out of her clothes, she couldn't help awareness that he was on the other side of the flimsy portal. He could technically barge back in at any time. Catch her while she dressed. Perhaps do more than that.

He could sweep her into his arms. Fall back with her on the bed. Kiss her and—

Sigh.

For a scientist, she had an overly active imagination. One she needed to rein in. The life she led didn't have room for a romantic, or even sexual, dalliance with a soldier. Too much was at stake.

And she wasn't just talking about her job and career.

As she booted up her laptop and used the many levels of encryption to access the secure forum where she chatted with members of the cyborg resistance, she reminded herself of why she had this job and why she'd taken the risk today of trying to smuggle some of the live nanos out.

I think there's no doubt now that somewhere in that building there is a living cyborg. A cyborg in need of rescue. As the mole, hidden and tunneling her way deeper and deeper, it was her job to inform the resistance of her findings. What she shouldn't be doing was anything that might get her fired such as getting a handsome soldier out of his pants and into hers.

My role as informant is more important than finding out if Adam prefers boxers or briefs.

CHAPTER EIGHT

A scratch indeed. Adam poked at the hole that went through his uniform shirt. At least the dark material and Laura's blurry eyesight meant she didn't grasp what had truly happened.

The bullet didn't miss. It entered his arm, and never exited. It never would. The missile, broken down by the nano bots and absorbed by his body, wouldn't leave behind any evidence. As a matter of fact, his arm bore only a slight pink pucker to show he'd gotten injured at all.

However, he couldn't hide the hole in his long sleeve. Given her observant nature, she'd possibly notice, so he shucked the damning evidence and balled it up. His white undershirt would do for the moment.

Disposing of it though meant he needed to perform more cover-up. In her guest bath, he located a first aid kit under the sink and slapped a large Band-Aid on for appearance's sake.

As he did all this, his BCI sent wireless pings out, checking on the surroundings as best he could. Without his usual cameras, he felt blind. Anyone could sneak up on him here, or listen in. It meant the message he texted to Rosalind had to rely on careful wording to convey the change in his schedule.

Gonna have to reschedule that beer for later. Working late. Can you pop by the house and make sure my guests are comfortable and give them my apologies? I seem to have lost A's

number.

Benign enough, but Rosalind would read the subtext which was,

Forget planning anything tonight. My fucking boss is making me work overtime. Make sure Anastasia and the others don't get into any trouble. Even better, don't let them do anything. I don't dare contact her myself in case her phone isn't secure.

What irked even more than not being to further their plan to infiltrate the factory was the fact he'd miss his weekly communication with his inside informant.

Calling themselves Talpa, which was Latin for mole, they'd begun receiving messages from the mystery insider about twenty-nine months ago. The first few messages were publicly left on a forum known to show sympathy for the cyborg cause. Initially they'd just watched the posted messages and not replied. Most people on the Freedom for Cyborgs forums were talkers, not acters. It was easy to spout support and make claims within the anonymity provided by the Internet.

Rosalind easily managed to weed out the basement dwellers and wannabe's from the real resistance fighters.

And Talpa was real.

The information they posted proved spot on and had so far led to at least a half-dozen cyborg rescues. Almost better numbers than Adam and his gang had managed on their own.

But now Talpa had embarked on an even more dangerous mission. Like Adam, their mysterious informant was working somewhere within CyberGlys. Who they were and in what capacity they didn't know.

They did try to find out, though.

Rosalind searched. She followed the IP addresses through proxies and firewalls, everywhere they led, only to come up empty-handed. Whoever they dealt with knew how to hide.

Kind of like his doctor who'd yet to come out of her room.

What did she do in there?

She'd claimed a need to change into something more comfortable. A more forward male might have said don't bother putting anything on at all. Then again, the element of discovery that came from peeling layers of clothes from a curvy body—

What the fuck? As he stood there like a raw recruit fantasizing, his mind finally smacked him awake and informed him that the doc was typing. To whom. About what.

Is she calling her boyfriend? He had no right to feel jealousy, and yet, it flared to life. He told it to stand down. Perhaps she simply replied to some emails. Or was talking via video chat to family or friends.

He tapped into her home network, only to get bounced back.

Strange. Most personal networks were barely encrypted, but then again, she did work for the government.

He probed at the wireless signal, but it buzzed discordantly, unwilling to let him in. Well, there was more than one way to eavesdrop on a binary conversation.

While he doubted he'd find a network connection in her bathroom, exiting it, he searched for her television, which wasn't readily apparent. Opening a large armoire tucked between a pair of windows, which gave a stunning view of the city, he noted a decent sound system, but no TV. As he rotated around, he discovered, to his shock, she didn't have a television at all.

Thus when she did finally exit her bedroom, was it any surprise he blurted, "How can you not have a television in your living room?"

"Because I don't need one."

"Don't need one?" He practically sputtered the words, his disbelief overwhelming. "But what do you do to entertain yourself? How do you play video games? Watch movies?" While it should be noted, he could technically do all these things wirelessly, there was a tactile enjoyment in flopping in a comfortable chair or couch and munching on dietary useless carbs while visually enjoying the antics of good cinema or challenging his dexterous skills as he manipulated a video game controller.

"I work most of the time, and when I'm not working, or researching, I'm sleeping."

"Surely you do something for relaxation? Your entire life can't revolve around the lab?"

"I like my work, but if you must know, I do also like to read." At his raised brow, she blushed, the pink in her cheeks enticing. "Non-fiction books usually about my work."

"But what about having fun?" As she shifted her stance, adopting a defensive posture, he realized how his accusation might sound. *I just accused her of being boring.*

"Who says I'm not enjoying myself?"

"Me. Don't forget, I've been watching you for some time now, and with the exception of tonight, when the director left you that mysterious cooler, your heart rate has never spiked, your eyes haven't shone with excitement, and I've certainly never heard you laugh."

"How would you know if my heart beats faster? For all you know, I'm in a constant adrenaline rush when I'm working. I'm a scientist. I get a kick out of discovery."

A snort escaped him. "What a load of crap."

Spine straight, she fixed him with a glare. "Would you mind not insulting me in my own home? What business is it of yours anyhow how I entertain myself?"

"It's none of my business. But I'd hate to think you're missing out."

"Missing out? On what? Fictional creations about absurd situations?"

"Forget television for a moment. What about the simple rush you get out of doing something for pleasure? Like hiking up a scenic mountain. Scuba diving and observing the beauty of nature on a coral reef." Things that even he, with his analytical mind, could appreciate. "What about the enjoyment that comes out of sharing an adventure with a friend, or a *lover...*" Why was it, when it came to Doctor Laura, his mind always revolved back to more intimate matters? She drew him like no other.

Her expression turned sad for a moment before tightening. "My work is important. Time enough later for me to indulge in frivolous activities."

"Or you could squeeze time in for them now."

"Says the guy assigned to watch over me. Don't tell me you think us going out to paint the town red is a good idea, given the threat supposedly to CyberGlys employees."

"You don't have to go out to have fun."

"So what do you propose we do? Play a board game? Cards?"

"I've got something better than that." Before she could question him some more, he showed her what he meant.

Reeling her into his arms didn't take any thought, or weighing of the pros and cons of his actions. He'd wanted to kiss her all evening. Weeks even. Pretty much from the first moment he'd begun observing her he'd wanted to see if her lush lips would prove pliant under his.

They were. Soft and welcoming.

For so long, he'd wanted to draw her against him and see how she molded to his frame.

She fit perfectly, her lush curves a perfect complement to his hard body.

He'd wanted to see if, beneath her prim and serious exterior, there lurked passion.

By all the nanos in his body, she practically melted him with the heat she unleashed with just one long, and sensual, kiss.

With his senses tingling, their lips separated, and they stared at each other, her bright brown eyes behind her glasses meeting his gaze with wonder. A wonder he understood. Her breath, already coming faster, brushed warmly against him.

The moment stretched, fraught with anticipation and desire. The cognitive part of his brain suggested he step away. Getting involved with the doctor, however pleasurable, wasn't part of his mission. It could prove a danger, especially given her scientific background. What if she recognized what he was? She could jeopardize more than his life. It was an unacceptable risk.

And yet…

The man within said fuck it.

He crushed her to him, his arms wrapping around her tight, his mouth claiming hers with intensity and determination. *She will know excitement.*

Already her heart raced. It pounded, the blood in her coursing frantically as it brought all of her nerves alive. At the same time, her body went limp in his arms, a languorous arousal weakening her muscles. But she needn't fear falling.

I have her, and I'm not letting go. I will show her pleasure. With me. And only me.

He could no more help the possessive feelings than he could resist her allure.

Her desire for him rose in a musky perfume, the layers of clothes separating them, unable to hide the evidence, not with his enhanced senses.

It served only to heighten his arousal. Hard. Harder than the steel they'd strengthened his bones with. Harder than the locks on the firewalls guarding his electronic secrets. So hard…it hurt?

Pain wasn't something he needed to feel unless he chose to, yet with her, he let the agony of wanting her and holding back fill him. The wild urgency was intoxicating. Not ruled by programming or rational thought, he just felt. Felt on a level he'd not imagined.

It made him forget where he was, who he was, and the danger his very existence posed. But lucky for them both, he was capable of faster-than-human reaction because, when the window shattered, he knew enough to spin his body and present his back in the split second before the deadly shards blasted them.

But more ominous than the deadly rain of glass was the thump and ticking of the metallic ball with its flashing red warning.

A bomb. Ah, hell.

No time to explain. No time for anything except escape. Bundling her over a shoulder and ignoring her scared query of "What's happening?" he charged at the door, exiting her condo even as the ominous ticking got faster and faster.

If it weren't for his speed, he doubted either of them would have made it out alive from the condo. As it was, he'd barely lunged into the hall and to his left when the explosion rocked the building. The floor underfoot shook. Smoke billowed from the portal he'd just escaped, and the ominous crackle of flames let him know there was nothing for them behind.

Nothing but destruction.

Someone wants me dead. Me, or is it the doctor they're targeting? Either way, they needed out of here. Fast.

A quick glance at the elevator showed it two floors away and rising. Would it stop here and disgorge a team to check on results and finish them off?

He didn't stay to find out. While he could handle a lot of damage, the fragile female over his shoulder, body wracked with coughs from the smoke, wouldn't fare well against bullets.

Tearing down the hall, he ignored the various heads poking from doorways, all asking the same thing.

"What's going on? Is there a fire?"

He snarled, "Get back inside," a futile attempt to save them from a possible culling by a follow-up death squad. However, human curiosity meant they milled out in the hall, voices high-pitched with excitement as they debated the best course of action. He hit the stairwell just as the fire alarms finally began to peal, and yet their strident sound couldn't hide the screams and the ominously shouted words of, "Oh my god, they have guns," for him to realize he needed to move faster.

"Hold on tight and don't say a word," was the only warning she got before he clamped one arm even tighter over her suspended thighs as he vaulted over the railing, letting himself drop several stories before reaching out to grasp the bar of the landing leading to the fourth floor.

Why not go all the way to ground level? Because a properly organized operation would have men stationed on the door exiting the stairwell, waiting to pick off anybody who emerged.

Cyborgs, being more durable and eminently smarter, would have waited in the stairwell and aimed upward, shooting anything that moved. Casualties, especially of the innocent, were an unfortunate side effect of this method.

As he burst onto the fourth level, a firm and quick kick snapping the lock meant to prevent people from entering the building, not exiting, he took a moment to analyze his surroundings. Despite the lack of smoke on this floor, the alarms here blazed as well, which meant there were people thronging the hall, all asking the same useless questions.

Some spotted his partial military uniform and soot-covered countenance and naturally assumed he had the answers.

"What's going on? Are we supposed to evacuate?"

Given the more chaos the humans caused, the better chance he'd have at slipping notice, he did the responsible thing. "Get out! Fire! Use the stairs."

The fact that he sidled along the wall, in the opposite direction, seemed to pass unnoticed, except by one human, who'd, up to now, remained quiet.

"Adam, where are you going?" a raspy-voiced doctor asked.

"Out."

"Isn't out the other way?" she inquired much too calmly. Good and bad. Good because it made her easy to handle, bad because he'd wager, once the shock set in, things could get ugly. Histrionics weren't something his kind was really programmed to deal with.

"Not for us," was his enigmatic reply.

"What's that supposed to mean?"

He didn't immediately reply as he chose his moment when no one appeared to pay them any mind and slipped into a condo, whose door had been left ajar by a fleeing inhabitant.

Shutting the portal behind him, he dropped Laura to her feet and took a quick stock of their situation. The condo itself followed the same layout as the doc's. Small entranceway opening onto the living room area and open kitchen. He ignored the décor and zeroed in on the sliding glass doors leading to the balcony.

In case anyone was listening, he sent one brief mental shout, which included his coordinates.

If anyone's listening, I'm coming out hot. Hot and bloody. The second he could kind of fix. A row of jackets and sweaters, even some ball caps, hung on hooks by the door. He snagged the largest one, which was thankfully black. It wouldn't do anything to clean the blood from his back, but it would at least hide the damage from any cursory looks.

Given it wasn't exactly balmy outside, he tossed a smaller navy blue coat at the doc, who snagged it one-handed while the other hand shoved her glasses back up on her nose. She stared at him then the jacket she held.

"Put it on."

To his surprise, she obeyed his request without question, but that didn't stop her from asking and repeating others. "Where are we going? What's happening? Is this related to the threat on CyberGlys? Shouldn't we call for help?"

Having stepped over to the sliding glass doors, which he opened and dared a peek outside, he answered her over his shoulder. "Listen, Doc, I don't have time to play a thousand questions. You're just going to have to trust me to get us out of here alive. Can you do that?" He turned to face her.

For a moment she stared at him, vulnerable in the oversized coat, her hair straggling out from its ponytail, her cheeks smudged with soot and even spots of blood, his he'd wager since he didn't spot any fresh wounds on her.

It didn't take much deduction to read the fear in her gaze or the will it took to keep her trembling from turning into tears and hysteria.

She kept her spine straight and her tears in check. His doc was made of stern stuff. She might eschew adventure, but when it came into her life—and shit blowing apart—she took it in stride with a bravery he admired.

She nodded. Then gasped as he swung her into his arms. "Hold on tight," he advised. She wound her arms around his neck. "Oh, and don't look down."

As she opened her mouth to say, "Why?" he pressed a hard kiss on her lips. Maybe their last.

It all depended on timing.

And luck. Something cyborgs didn't truly believe in, but his human side was counting on it.

With one last mentally shouted, *Here we come,* Adam ran at the sliding glass doors.

CHAPTER NINE

Trust me, he says. Trust him to kill us both.

The screen door popped as Adam hit it and took them outside at a sprint. As Adam ran at the ledge rimming the outdoor balcony, she wanted to scream at him, but terror stole her voice. With a leap, he balanced on the parapet. Given their distance from the ground, she couldn't help but shut her eyes tight.

This isn't happening. Maybe she dreamed. Maybe this was all a nightmare, a production of her overworked mind.

"Don't let go," he advised. As if she would. She clung tight to his neck, especially when one of his arms moved away from her upper body, leaving only a single one to support her legs. Forget further warning or time to prepare, or protest. He jumped, and they were airborne.

Oh my god—who probably wasn't listening, given she'd written a thesis disproving his existence—*we're going to die.*

Her head snapped as their descent was abruptly halted. Given the screams and sirens and the air whistling by her head, they weren't dead. Yet.

She opened one eye to peek.

It appeared they were floating or flying or something because they certainly weren't standing on solid ground—which she intended to kiss if she made it out of this insanity alive. The odds truly weren't in favor of survival, not given they hung suspended at least two stories or more in the air.

Using only one hand, Adam held on to a braided cable, displaying a strength she hoped wouldn't fail them, especially since it seemed his one-armed hold on the dangling rope was the only thing keeping them from crashing and splatting much like overripe fruit.

As they swung through the air, a pendulum without a clock, she tried to take in what happened around them. Over Adam's shoulder, bedlam reigned. It didn't take a genius to guess that the smoke billowing from a floor a few levels up and now a block away, given their movement, was her condo. It also didn't take someone with a Mensa level IQ to realize that the figures dangling from rappelling ropes on her building had spotted them and now aimed weapons their way.

Not sure how announcing it would help them in any way, but feeling a need to let him know, she yelled, "Guns!"

"Fuck," was his reply, which really didn't reassure. "Crank us faster," he hollered to someone above them. Had she neglected to mention the rope they dangled from was anchored to a helicopter, whose timing was impeccable?

Forget kissing the ground. She should kiss the chopper pilot first. The military had come to their rescue. So quickly? But how had they known? Who cared? Their arrival had saved them from painting the sidewalk red.

A jerk on the rope sent them spinning. She bit her tongue lest she scream again. They ascended more quickly and just in time, too, as cracks sounded behind them.

They're shooting! At least she assumed that was what the sound meant, a hypothesis confirmed when a missile whistled way too close to her ear.

"Tuck your head into my shoulder," Adam shouted, his words barely distinct over the roaring stutter of the chopper blades.

Face buried against his neck, she couldn't help but note how Adam kept his body turned so that any more bullets would hit him first. Once again, he played the part of human shield.

Or did he?

With terror threatening to freeze her mind, she let it wander in a direction other than the danger they faced—why dwell on the possibility they could plummet to their deaths at any moment and force the medical examiner to turn to DNA for identification? Why worry about the possibility some determined shooters would turn them into the human equivalent of Swiss cheese when she had a more interesting thing to focus on?

Adam.

Sexy Adam, who kissed her and made a mockery of her dull existence with just one touch.

Gentlemanly Adam, who protected her, even though it caused him great injury.

Strong Adam, who carted her out of the danger zone and never even broke a sweat.

Crazy Adam, who jumped off a bloody balcony and, in a stroke of timing, caught a rescue rope.

Not human Adam, WHO WAS A FREAKING CYBORG!

Okay, so she shouted the last bit mentally. It didn't make the revelation any less stunning.

All this time, she'd looked for evidence of cyborgs at CyberGlys, only to have one under her very nose. In her condo. Working for the military.

The traitor.

How could he knowingly work for the men who'd ordered the slaughter of hundreds of his kind? Or did he not have a choice? Was he a reprogrammed model who couldn't think for himself? Had he gained freedom only to lose his humanity again as the military plugged holes in their cybernetic units? Did he willingly choose to align himself against the others in order to survive? Or was he a new model, an improved one that no one suspected existed?

She'd have to figure it out later. They'd reached the end of their journey. Reeled to the edge of a helicopter, Laura only had a second to note a set of hands reached out to haul her in. A really strong woman's hands, while a male set yanked Adam into relative safety.

Laura, the shock of the past moments making her legs unresponsive, sat in an unladylike heap on the floor of the chopper and stared at her rescuers. A statuesque blonde, who could have modeled for any fashion magazine, as could have the stunning male at her side. If she hadn't already met Adam—and kissed him—she might have found herself more in awe of his looks. Blond, built, with a chiseled face and body, he was much too handsome to be real.

Dressed in black from head to toe, they didn't look like soldiers. They didn't look like robots either. But she had a niggling suspicion.

She'd blame shock for blurting out, "Are you all cyborgs?"

They exchanged looks, silent ones, and yet she could have sworn they spoke. Heck, they probably did. Most models had a wireless capability for communication. It was how the military conveyed orders and downloaded programming changes.

Just when it seemed as if no one would reply, Adam shook his head and broke the silence. "She's seen too much for me to easily explain it away."

"You mean like the fact that you move faster than is biologically possible, how your back has already healed from the cuts, and, yes, I noticed that. Kind of hard not to, given you had me tossed over your shoulder with only one thing to stare at." Well, two, but given the situation, ogling his ass didn't seem appropriate.

"You do realize that by letting her in on the secret, you're jeopardizing us all."

With a weary expression that she wouldn't have thought a machine capable of, but then again, cyborgs weren't only machines, Adam scrubbed a hand over his face. "I know. But what else was I supposed to do? I couldn't let her die."

Ah, how sweet. She couldn't help the warmth that spread through her at his words. Quickly followed by a chill at the reply from his companions.

"It might have been better if you had. Someone was really keen on having her killed. Why do you think we were in the area, close enough to catch your distress call?"

"I wasn't distressed," Adam protested. "Merely inconvenienced. If I were alone, I could have handled the situation."

"At what expense?" the other male pointed out. "Innocents would have gotten killed."

A grimace twisted Adam's countenance. "Innocents have probably already died tonight, but not through any fault of mine. Whoever came after us was determined and didn't seem to care about casualties or drawing notice. You never did say how you knew to be in the area though."

"Rosalind caught wind from one of her informants about a planned attack on the doctor's condo, and we went on the move."

"A good thing you did. I wasn't looking forward to dodging them on the ground and making my way to one of the safe houses unnoticed."

"Again, all things you could have done easily had you chosen to leave her behind."

Laura couldn't help but shiver. *Thank goodness Adam doesn't share the same opinion as this lady, or I'd be dead.*

Once again, he came to her defense. "If I'd left her behind, they would have killed her, or worse."

What was worse than death?

"Then you should have disposed of her so she couldn't give away any secrets before escaping. Instead, we had to swoop in and save your ass, quite publicly I might add."

The handsome male laughed. "We'll be YouTube sensations before the night is out."

"I'll have Rosalind scrub any pictures or videos she finds," Adam replied.

"Who's Rosalind?" Too late, Laura wished she'd bitten her tongue, as the blonde woman turned her cold gaze and attention her way.

"What's done is done. Perhaps you were right in saving her. She might have answers for us. After all, the attack seemed geared toward her. But the question is why? What makes her so important that anyone, even a fringe group, would so publicly and violently attack with no regard for civilian casualty? This isn't how things usually work."

"Instead of focusing on why, perhaps we should be asking who?" the other male interjected, lounging in a seat, but eschewing the buckles.

Adam, in the process of peeling out of his stolen coat, frowned. "What do you mean who? Didn't you say Rosalind had an informant notify her? That must mean she knows who's responsible for the attack."

"Nope. It was a rapidly organized mercenary hit. Although, given the weaponry and organization, I have to wonder if it was military in origin."

"Secret ops?"

"Most likely. Which means your little doctor here is obviously in possession of something they deem valuable. Question is, what is it?"

Finding herself the focus of all their gazes wasn't reassuring. Laura, still seated on the vibrating floor, hugged her knees to her chest. Time to remind them she existed and had feelings. First though, she poked the glasses she'd not yet lost up on her nose. "If they were looking for something, then why blow up my apartment? Wouldn't it have made more sense to search it?"

"So it's not a physical object they seek. What are you hiding in that human brain of yours?"

Given the way the female stared at her with her head on a tilt, she wouldn't put it past her to demand to dissect it. Laura shivered, and Adam frowned.

"Anastasia, would you stop trying to frighten her? She's not the enemy. On the contrary, if the military, or even an unknown faction, want her dead so badly, then obviously she knows something of worth. Even if she doesn't realize what it is."

"Why would the military want me dead? That makes no sense. I work for them. They assigned you as my guard to keep me safe."

"A good thing they chose Adam too. Anyone

else and you'd be barbecued meat right now," the other male cyborg said.

"Seth! Must you be so crude?" This time the woman took offense, and Laura relaxed a bit. "You know I'm hungry. So much for having a real Earth-cooked dinner tonight." And with those words, Laura tensed back up.

"Sorry. I guess you'll have to make do with whatever we can scrounge up."

Anastasia made a face. "Oh yay. More rocks and plants. You know, just because we can digest and make use of the compounds in raw materials doesn't make it all right. I see nothing wrong with enjoying a flavorful meal, one that engages my taste buds."

"I've got something you can taste." The leer on Seth's face did not need interpretation.

As Laura blushed and ducked her gaze, Anastasia exclaimed, "Seth," again, but this time in fond exasperation.

"What am I going to do with you, husband?"

"Hopefully chapters nine through thirteen of that tantric book I downloaded."

"Ahem, while I am usually the first to offer a video camera to tape kinky sex, I think we do have more important matters to attend to. Such as where the fuck do we go next? If we assume the target is Doctor Cowen—"

How impersonal, Laura thought, a little miffed at Adam's formal tone.

"—then my place should provide a safe hideaway while we regroup and plan. If, however, the military is behind it—"

"Then we should hurry back to your place so we can be on hand to greet any guests," said Seth with a bright grin, not at all perturbed at his desire to rush into danger.

An indication of faulty programming? Or was this what happened when the emotions of a testosterone-filled male mixed with the almost invincible nature of a cyborg?

A frown marred Adam's face. "They better not blow up my house. I've got some priceless shit inside."

Anastasia snickered. "Yeah, like your collection of vintage *Star Trek* figures. I still find your fascination with the Borg disturbing."

"Funny because I would have thought you were more disturbed by the Seven of Nine costume I made you wear that one time."

The punch Seth threw at Adam just barely missed his jaw, but his simmering jealousy was evident for all.

Adam and Anastasia used to date? Odd how Seth wasn't the only one who felt an urge to slap something. Laura fought to keep a scowl from her lips as Anastasia laughed.

"Oh my god. That stupid costume. I still can't believe I agreed to wear that thing to that Halloween party."

"I can't believe we're still talking about it," Seth grumbled with arms crossed over his chest and his lower lip jutting.

"Don't pout. It was a long time ago. If it makes you feel any better, I've got a much better costume in mind for you. It's so indecent I doubt you'll let me wear it in public. I got the idea from a certain movie you forced me to watch." Anastasia winked at Seth, whose irritation melted in an instant.

"The force is with me!" Seth exclaimed.

Listening to the banter, Laura really had to wonder how the cyborgs managed any kind of revolution. Were they always so playful and unheeding of the danger around them? "Are your kind ever serious?"

Anastasia's lips tightened. "Our *kind* is too serious by far."

"I'm sorry. I didn't mean to sound insulting. It's just, here we are, on the run from who knows what forces, and Adam is injured. He doesn't know if people are out to kill him, or me, or both of us, and yet you're joking about Halloween costumes. I'll admit, I've not had much experience with cyborgs, but I kind of expected—"

"Less emotion, more robot?" Adam fixed her with a stare that clearly displayed his disappointment. It seemed he'd taken her words as a direct insult. Yet she'd not meant it that way. If only she could tell him she felt sorry for his kind. Thought they'd gotten the raw end of a deal. That she wanted only to help them. But faced with disapproving glares, Laura clamped her lips shut and sat huddled on the floor.

The laughter and banter stopped though. All oral communication did. Oh, she was sure they *spoke*, just not to her. She wasn't part of the group.

Because I am human. Their enemy.

CHAPTER TEN

The female is right. We are letting our human emotions overrule our common sense. Anastasia, always so mission focused, was the first to bring them back on track. *A plan of action is required.*

Do we dare contact Rosalind? Adam projected his query, even as he wondered if it was safe to do so. Their mind-to-mind communication worked best in close proximity. While it was possible to ride certain wave signals, cellphone ones being the easiest, there was a lack of encryption with that method, which meant their words could be heard if Big Brother was listening. But the cell phone frequency method wouldn't work with Rosalind.

Buried underground, the walls lined with lead and other signal-damping features, not even the strongest of radio waves could get through. Which meant he'd either have to contact her directly and possibly tip their hand as to her existence and whereabouts, post a message online and hope Rosalind saw it, or wait until she contacted them through a secure channel and advised them of the status of their situation.

A situation that currently boasted low survival probability rates. The longer they stayed in the air, the more likely they'd get spotted and possibly shot down. Or followed. They needed to land and get moving on foot. The sooner, the better.

Adam needed to know more in order to make a

decision. *Is that Murray piloting?*

Murray was actually one of their human recruits, but a loyal one. His brother had been one of the cyborgs brutally gunned down in the first of the culling waves. His poor brother, Cyrus, a vegetable from a skateboarding accident as a teenager, had been volunteered by his family for the cyborg project.

Despite his change, Murray loved his brother. When the media kept replaying the video of Cyrus, kneeling on the ground, hands over his head, offering no resistance, being killed by soldiers with a bullet to the head, Murray wanted to do something about it. Although he vetoed Adam's first plan of kill them all. He'd harbored a few anger issues back then.

Murray had a logic Adam wished more humans would adopt. "Every single cyborg is someone's brother or father or son. It's not their fault the military fucked up. They didn't have to kill them."

Without trial. Without mercy.

Of course, not all of humanity held that belief. Most were mindless sheep, swayed by the military and the media's portrayal of cyborgs as emotionless killing machines intent on wiping out humanity.

He especially liked the scare tactic that said cyborgs could infect humans with nanos and turn them into robots.

So untrue and yet the public gobbled it up. For a while, tin foil hats were all the craze, as marketing pros rode the merchandising wave.

Get your aluminum skull cap and keep the cyborgs from taking over your mind.

Bullshit. Just like the Cyber tasers were useless, and the anti-nanotech shots were a fantasy. Ignorance was so much easier to teach. And fear was contagious.

Murray is piloting, Anastasia confirmed. *Which means we now have two humans aboard to protect. What's the plan?*

Plan. His plan was to survive and not lose anyone. *We need to land before we're—*

The helicopter tilted to the side as something impacted it. He didn't need Murray's shouted, "Bogeys, two of them. They just popped up out of nowhere," to know they'd just run out of time.

How the fuck did we not hear them coming? Seth mentally exclaimed. *I'm not reading any radio signals on any frequency.*

Adam really hated it when the enemy came to a fight better equipped than him. *I really need to get some better toys.* But first they had to survive.

Anastasia and Seth, you grab Murray and get your asses to the rendezvous point. We'll plan to meet there for oh three hundred hours. If that spot is compromised, Ana, go to where we had our first coffee date at oh six when it opens.

What about you and the woman?

He and the doc were going to lead the enemy away from his friends. Anastasia was right. If they were after the doc, then she was a liability to the movement. He wouldn't jeopardize all he'd built because of some misfiring nanos that seemed unduly attached to a human female.

But that doesn't mean I won't do my best to save her sweet ass and find out who dares to try and kill her. Because if there was one thing cyborgs did well, and that none of their programming scrubs could erase, it was their efficiency when it came to dealing in death. Vengeance was their specialty.

CHAPTER ELEVEN

Laura watched with rounded eyes and no questions as Adam slid into the cockpit and a man emerged, only to stumble as the chopper bucked with yet another impact.

Someone is shooting at us. Which probably didn't bode well.

Cold air rushed into the passenger area as Seth opened the sliding door. It could mean only one thing.

"You're leaving?"

"Alas, we'll have to continue the party elsewhere. Murray, you are wearing a vest?"

The pilot, who could only be Murray, thumped his upper body. "Yup, but I sure hope you know what you're doing because I doubt it will stop me from painting the pavement if you miscalculate."

"As if I, with my higher cognitive abilities, would so erroneously misjudge something so trite as a suicide jump."

Judging by the pallor on the pilot's face, Laura wasn't the only one less than reassured.

Anastasia finished buckling into a harness, as did Seth, then, with the pilot in tow, they dove out the side with only a brief, "See you later if the odds are in your favor."

But the odds weren't, in her favor that was. Despite the dips and swerves, Adam swung the craft through thuds and pings, indicating pursuers hot on their tail.

When he emerged from the cockpit, she gaped at him as he shrugged into a harness and checked his holster with its tucked pistol.

"Who's driving?" she asked, afraid she knew the answer.

"Me."

She looked at him standing before her and then at the cockpit he'd just vacated.

He laughed. "Really I am, just wirelessly via the computer."

She really would have preferred a different answer. Call her old-fashioned, but she'd changed her stance on automated locomotion. Some things really needed a driver.

The craft shuddered, and a high pitched whine provided a worrisome soundtrack to go with their listing and obvious descent. "We're going to die, aren't we?" she said, rapidly losing optimism as they lost altitude.

"Not today. I hope." Not reassuring. He plucked her glasses and tucked them into a pocket. "I want you to straddle me. Legs around my waist, arms around my neck."

Given he seemed to have a plan, which was more than she had, Laura wrapped herself around him, koala style.

"You know, if circumstances were different, and we were wearing fewer clothes, this could be a lot of fun," he teased. His attempt at levity didn't relax her, especially since some bullets whizzed past them through the open door.

With a squeak, she buried her face in his neck. At least if she died, she didn't have to see it coming.

"Ever sky dived?" he asked.

"Nope."

"Me either but it sounds like fun. Whatever you do, don't let go."

It was the only warning she got before he darted toward the opening. Screaming, because the situation sure as hell warranted it, they plummeted, cold air rushing past her face, buffeting her against him so that holding on proved easy.

She heard a rippling sound, as of canvas stretched. Daring to peek with one eye, she noted the harness he'd put on, while not sporting a parachute, gave him wings. Fabric stretched between his arms and body, buoying them, much as air currents floated birds.

But they weren't birds, and he wasn't flapping any wings. So down they went still, faster than she liked, but better than the fiery alternative.

For the second time that day, something exploded, their chopper, as it gave up its fight to stay aloft and crashed to the ground in the distance, a bright fireball exploding in the night.

More ominous than its brilliant flaring glare or billowing smoke though was the sound of helicopters still searching the night sky.

She could see bright beams crisscrossing, sweeping the area looking for survivors.

Looking for us.

Adam tilted his arms and angled them away from the searchers, taking them away from the lights into pure darkness. During their short flight, they'd exited the city and were now in the suburbs, where housing developments sprang up in clusters but still left swatches of land untouched, virgin soil for bulldozers. Would she and Adam be fertilizer for weeds when dawn crested?

Nope.

Try food for fishies.

"Take a deep breath," he advised. "And don't let go."

Good thing he warned her because when they hit the water her first impulse was to open her mouth and scream. Given drowning didn't seem conducive to her health, she kept her lips clamped.

The shock of the cold though, not to mention panic, didn't make it easy. Yes, he'd told her to hold on tight, but dammit, he was sinking.

And bringing her with him!

She let go and thrashed, bogged down by the layers of clothes and, with the dark water all around, quickly lost sense of direction.

Where was up?

Did she sink down?

Blowing out a little air, she tried to see which direction the bubbles went. She failed. Blinded, she couldn't tell which way to swim. She blew again to no avail. All she managed to do was amplify the tightness in her lungs.

Yet she felt no real pain. As a matter of fact, lethargy imbued her limbs, a numbness from the cold temperature. *Lucky me, I don't feel a thing at all.*

The one thing that did scream from pressure was her lungs. They wanted air. Needed oxygen. Needed relief.

She tried to hold it in. Tried to ignore her body's demand. She failed.

She exhaled her last breath.

CHAPTER TWELVE

Dammit. He'd told her to hold on, and Laura had, until they hit the water and sank. Human self-preservation had kicked in at that point—for her at any rate. To him, water was just a medium like air or the void of space. In her case, though, she didn't have the ability to survive long underwater, and in her attempt to save herself, she flailed away from him.

Given his hands were busy as he shucked his soggy wings, more weight than he could easily handle right now given the drag, he couldn't spare a hand to clamp her to him.

As soon as he'd shed as much as he could, though, his first priority was to reclaim her, if he could find her.

Despite the protective film the nanos dropped over his eyes, he couldn't see much. Given his orbs were still mostly organic, he couldn't illuminate his field of vision. The murk blinded and he found his movements hampered by the current. He couldn't spot Laura.

Logic insisted she'd probably sink rather than float, given she'd entered the river fully dressed. Without pausing to take a breath, he dove down, his nanos capable of filtering the oxygen from the water, not that he needed much. A handy cyborg trait meant their pores could absorb needed chemicals and gases. In this case, oxygen. There was no discomfort in holding his breath. No panic. He could stop breathing for weeks, even months.

Laura couldn't, and she had to be getting short on air.

The very idea she might die drowning while in his care galvanized him. Adam swam, arms sweeping in wide arcs, seeking even just the most minute of touch or clue.

A tickle against his jaw. Not a fish or vegetation, but rather a string of bubbles, bubbles he hoped meant Laura. He sank, arms to his side, projecting himself much like an anchor, moving so fast he almost shot past her, only the wet tendrils of her hair brushing his face warning him of her presence.

Halting his momentum, he drew her to him as close as he could, so close that when she exhaled her final breath, he felt the air on his lips. Before she could inhale, he pressed his mouth to hers and blew.

At first she did not respond, and so he breathed for her. Blow in, giving her rich oxygen. Suck, ridding her of carbon dioxide. As he pumped air into her lungs, he kept one arm anchored about her waist while his free arm and legs moved in powerful flutter kicks and an arm stroke that propelled them upward.

Their heads broke the surface of the water, but Adam did not immediately remove his lips, even though he no longer breathed for her. Laura now took slow, shuddering inhalations. Her heart rate, while slow, still beat. He hugged her tight, needing the contact, wanting the reassurance that she lived.

The fear, the panic when he'd thought her lost, possibly dying, wasn't something he cared to re-experience. It was bad enough his memory banks had stored the event in all its frightening glory for him to relive at will.

How could the fate of one affect him so? Since when did he care so deeply if someone lived or died?

Not just anyone though. Laura.

A human woman who'd come to mean something to him as he observed her and now, finally, got to know her.

But he wouldn't know her for long if he didn't get his partially metal ass moving.

Given the coldness of her limbs, he realized they couldn't remain in the water. Already she probably suffered from hypothermia, the water cool enough to reduce her core temperature. As his feet hit the rocky shoals of the river bank, he swung her into his arms and strode out of the water.

She shivered in his grip, her teeth chattering, her entire body a tremble. The gray pallor of her skin and the deep mauve of her lips worried him.

"We need to get you warm," he spoke aloud, seeking to reassure not just her but himself. To his surprise, she replied, showing more spirit than he'd have expected given her near drowning.

"N-n-no duh," she said with a stutter. "W-w-we need t-t-t-o strip, t-too."

"Getting naked. Great idea," he teased and was rewarded with a wan smile.

Despite the irrationality of the action, because it did nothing, after all, to further his mission, lightening the moment was all he could provide Laura with until he found them somewhere to shelter safely. Remaining in the open wasn't an option, not with the helicopters still searching in the distance.

Not for long he'd wager, though. Already he could see lights in the distance, more choppers put in the air by rabid news stations looking for more video footage to boost their ratings.

Inwardly, he cringed to think of the number of cell phone clips taken of his balcony jump and wild escape in the city. Then again, the darkness, the hour, and unexpected action of it might have gotten missed with all the other excitement going on.

A problem to worry about later.

This close to the city, the river bank, while vacant seeming, wasn't exactly unclaimed. They'd washed ashore on an uninhabited location, parkland used by residents and tourists alike. This meant there were trails and a parking lot, unlit this time of night. What it also meant was no vacant vacation cottages or, hell, even a proper house he could commandeer.

The most secure building he came across stored maintenance supplies, but it was the best he could do for the moment.

Purple lips, chattering teeth, and clammy skin, one look at Laura and he knew she required immediate attention.

The building lock couldn't withstand a firmly placed kick. It popped open, and he carried her inside, shutting the door behind him. Lucky for him, the light switch worked. He flicked it on and peeked around at his options. They didn't amount to much. A rusted lawnmower, gas powered and sitting beside an equally aging trimmer. A few rakes against the wall. Some shovels. Signs. *No swimming. Utility vehicles forbidden on the trails.*

None of those were of any use, but he did spot one cobwebbed corner with promise. A pile of burlap sacks, dusty and musty, used to protect some of the more fragile saplings from the rough winters, but as fine a bed as he could hope for. It sure beat the concrete floor.

He laid a shivering Laura on the rough, woven fabric then deftly stripped her of her sodden clothes, his hands efficient but still noting the softness of her skin. The dire situation might have kept his usual ardor for her under control, but it certainly did nothing for his powers of observation.

Though he'd seen her nude before, once again, he found himself captivated by the beauty of her, from the tiny imperfections like the scar above her hip from an appendectomy to the lushness of her frame, her belly rounded and soft, her waist indented while her hips flared.

He closed his eyes against her alluring nudity, aghast he would even look upon her like this when she so desperately needed his help. Hanging her clothes upon the tines of the lawn rakes leaning against the walls, he also disposed of his own damp outerwear. He made sure to place his pistol, which hopefully had survived its wet plunge, within arm's reach before he crowded in beside her and pulled her into his arms.

He couldn't help the thrill of holding her naked in his arms, but he didn't do it for perverse reasons. Even he, the corrupt machine, had morals. He did this to save her life.

Everyone knew the basics of survival. Skin-to-skin provided the best method of warming a person, even better if that person was cyborg and capable of regulating his core temperature. Bit by bit, Adam raised his heat level, imparting as much of himself as he could, his cocoon embrace covering a lot of her body.

Her shivers eased as he held her, his slowly increasing warmth seeping into her chilly limbs.

She squirmed a little against him, her head

tucking more firmly under his chin, her hands coming to rest on his chest. Over his heart, which beat steadily. A surprise since he'd forgotten to breathe once she moved.

She sighed, the soft puff of air feather-light on his chest.

"How are you feeling?"

"Surprised."

Not the answer he expected. Scared, yes. Tired, probably. In shock, normal. But..."Surprised? By what?"

"The fact we're alive."

"Of course we are. There was never any other possible outcome." Another cybernetic failure, one most cyborgs suffered from—overconfidence.

She chuckled, the sound raw and raspy, not surprising given her evening. "You know, when you advised me I needed more excitement in my life, I certainly never expected things would turn out this way."

"I always knew we'd end up naked together," he teased.

Interesting how his claim helped her core temperature rise a degree. Nice to know just his words could have an effect on his lovely doc.

"I wasn't talking about—I mean—" she sputtered, and given how hot her cheek became against his chest, he knew she blushed.

"Are you going to tell me you didn't think about it?"

"I did." Shyly admitted. "But fantasizing doesn't mean I actually thought we would."

"And now that we are skin to skin, and alone?" He stroked fingers up and down her spine, slowly, softly.

"It's nice."

His fingers stopped. "Just nice?" Yes, his pride demanded he ask.

She laughed. "Very nice, especially now that no one is shooting at us and we're not drowning."

"We've had a bit of an eventful evening."

She snorted. "You call that a bit?"

"I'm a cyborg. We're always living on the edge."

"There's the edge, and then there was tonight. Is it always like this for you? For cyborgs? The people trying to kill you and the violence, and...just everything?"

"Me personally? No. Not for a long time." His layers of cover kept him safely insulated. "But others of my kind... Some live constantly under threat. Many have to fight, and of those who do, more don't survive."

"So you're aware of their plight?" she asked, her breath soft and warm against his chest, the tremors of her flesh gone.

"Of course I'm aware. All cyborgs know of the struggle we face daily. The persecution."

"And yet you work for the military. You work for the cyborg enemy."

She thought him a traitor? A human male might have taken offense that she thought him with so little honor. However, he could see how this would look logically from the outside. His turn to laugh. "Undercover as an agent for the resistance." No point in hiding it. Laura had already seen and heard too much. At this point, he either trusted her with his secrets and drew her into the group, or he killed her. He really hoped for the former. "I would never willingly aid the military against my kind. But I will do what I have to in order to liberate others of my kind who have fallen into their traps."

"But how? How did you pass their screening? How have you fooled them for so long?"

"Great programming. Even better hacking." And luck. An unquantifiable denominator he'd enjoyed so far. "I've worked very hard to make sure they never know what I am. I have no urge to die."

"And yet you technically risk your life every day when you go to work."

"Because I must. I can't just sit back knowing there are others out there not as lucky as me. I have to help them. Have to see if I can't find a way to make the military stop hunting us, exterminating us, and using us."

"Can they still force you to do what they command? I thought the uprising meant you didn't have to obey anymore."

He almost shuddered at the reminder of life before the grand revelation. A life, or unlife, where his actions were governed by another. Where he was simply a puppet, existing at the whim of another. "We've wiped the military programming as best we can, but there's so much about ourselves we don't know. It is believed that if we can discover our origins, figure out the method of creation, that we can ensure we never become slaves or victims again."

"You say victim. Are you all victims? I know when the program first rolled out, the military claimed the cyborgs were volunteers only."

"Untrue. Most did not choose this. I never would have." Although now, even with the hardship he'd faced, given the alternative of his past human existence, being a cyborg wasn't so bad.

"So you were one of the victims?"

Perhaps long ago. Now he was a survivor and a leader. "Why so many questions? Wait, what am I asking? I should be more worried if you weren't bombarding me with queries."

He could almost feel her rueful smile against his skin. "I guess I do question a lot. I've always been curious. I realize this sounds horrible to admit, but cyborgs have always fascinated me. I've always wanted to know more about your kind. So many things don't add up. The media claims, video footage I've seen. Stories I've heard. I know you're not the monsters the media portrays you as. I know you're human at the core. But how much of you was changed? What makes you so different? The technology…" she trailed off.

"What about the technology?"

"It's going to sound silly. I shouldn't say it."

"Tell me."

"Science isn't advanced enough for the capabilities you've displayed. Humanity doesn't know enough to create the things that make you special. This is going to sound nuts, but I think the nanotechnology isn't—" She paused. "Isn't—"

He finished her sentence. "One hundred percent human?"

She stiffened in surprise. "You mean you already suspected a non-earth-based origin to your creation?"

"Yes, but only recently and, to my embarrassment, I must admit, only by chance."

As if his admission was the key to unlock her, Laura admitted, "You know the stuff I've been working with in the lab? I'm pretty sure it's from a cyborg."

"I know."

"You do?" She craned to peek at him, the clarity

in her eyes returning, her face so vulnerable without her glasses.

"Why do you think I got myself assigned to your lab? We suspect CyberGlys is harboring cyborgs. Perhaps even the secret of our making."

"If they are, it's on the lower levels where the security is truly tight."

"Have you ever been?"

Her nose rubbed against his chest as she shook her head. "No. I don't have the clearance. I don't know of anyone who does."

Her jaw cracked as she yawned, fatigue overtaking her, but it was a natural tiredness that came from a day full of exertion. He let her drift off. They had hours before they needed to make the rendezvous point. Hours for him to plot. Plan. Feel. Touch. Torture himself.

With her skin, warm and dewy against his, her temperature almost back to normal, and the danger for the moment at bay, he couldn't stop himself from swelling against her lower belly. For too long he'd tried to control his attraction to her, but machine or not, at the core, he was still a man.

A man who couldn't help but want her.

Yet the real question was, despite her seeming acceptance of his cyborg heritage, would she want him, too?

CHAPTER THIRTEEN

Despite her fascination with Adam's admissions and openness, lethargy dragged Laura down. Extreme fatigue, though, didn't mean a dreamless sleep.

Once again, she found herself in the lab. That stupid, awful lab that she'd come to hate yet couldn't seem to escape.

Despite knowing what would happen, she couldn't stop it.

Shots were fired. *Bang. Bang.*

In came—

Hold on, it wasn't CG311 this time who ghosted through her dream. Dressed just like a campus guard, Adam entered the room.

She strayed from her memorized script with a gasped, "What are you doing here? You can't be here. You have to run. Run, dammit, before you die."

But it was as if he didn't hear her. Caught in the horrific loop of her nightmare, he repeated the words she'd come to hate.

"You need to hide."

Hide. There was nowhere to hide. Nowhere to run. Even her own mind didn't provide safety.

Adam spun as soldiers crowded the door, their weapons aimed with deadly intent.

Most times, at this point in her dream, she was frozen. She knew what was coming. Wanted to stop it. Shout at them to go away. To change the course of things.

But every time, she stood mute. Paralyzed.

Every time but now.

Now it was Adam facing the firing squad. Adam lacing his hands over his head.

She dashed toward danger, throwing herself before him. "No. Don't shoot. You can't. It's not his fault. He doesn't deserve to die."

The masked soldiers didn't reply. Nor did their weapons lower.

Strong hands spun her. A rough finger tilted her head until she faced Adam.

"You can't stop this, Doc."

"There must be a way."

"Not for me. Not for any of us." His blue eyes were clear and resigned.

As he kissed her, she clung to him, clung to him even as the soldiers opened fire and his body jerked in response.

And she screamed…and screamed…and…

Woke up to Adam shaking her, his tone worried. "Laura, wake up. It's just a nightmare. It's not real, just an emotional response brought on by the many shocks you've suffered."

"They killed you," she sobbed against him. "Shot you without even giving you a chance."

"No, they didn't. I'm here. I'm alive. I'm with you."

"For now. But what about when we leave? This world isn't safe here for you. For any of you."

"How about we worry about that later? Right now there's no danger. Unless you count a danger of me kissing you."

She angled her head and strove to see his features in the gloom through damp lashes. "How is a kiss dangerous?"

"Because I doubt I can stop at one."

"Oh." *Oh.*

His mouth slanted over hers and stole any further words or thoughts. He kissed her with a sweetness that had her hungry for more. Yes, she hungered. Hungered for him. She, too, didn't want to stop at one.

One kiss would not be enough. Neither would two. Or three.

Death could take him at any time. Take them both actually, given the turn her life had taken. Why waste this moment wondering the what-ifs? Why stop when they had this tiny moment in time to share something beautiful? Sensual.

While somewhat aware before of their proximity, she now truly paid attention. *It's just me and him, with no clothes, no interruptions, nothing to lose but a chance for pleasure.*

It was a pleasure to snuggle into his warm body. His chest was smooth, the velvet skin of it covering firm muscles, which flexed as she stroked fingers over them.

The hardness of his erection pressed against her lower belly, turgid and hot, his arousal unmistakable, and for her. *For me.* This handsome man, this guy who was special in so many ways desired her.

Such a heady feeling.

She boldly opened her mouth under his and let her tongue be the first to sashay forward. His groan vibrated against her lips and had her undulating her body against him. Big hands cupped her full bottom, drawing her mound more firmly against his shaft. Her turn to moan.

The folds of her sex were already slick with

desire, her body humming with need. While she would have enjoyed taking more time to explore, she knew that time was something they had precious little of.

She needed to seize the moment. Or, even better, seize him.

Grasping him around the base, she smiled against his mouth as he sucked in a breath finally.

"What are you doing?" he asked.

In between nibbles on his chin, she replied, "Having." She angled her hips so that the tip of him rubbed against her clit. "An amazing." She threw her leg over his hip, opening herself to him. "Adventure." She bit his lower lip as she drew him into her body.

His body jerked, his hips pistoning forward, driving him deeper. She moaned, the pleasure of him stretching her an absolute delight.

"I wanted our first time to be slower," he said as he thrust in and out of her. "I had plans for your body. Great plans. Fun plans."

Clutching his nape with fingers that dug into his skin, her breath coming in pants, she said, "Save it for the next time. I just need you."

At her words, he rolled onto his back and drew her atop him, still connected, still thrusting. He drew her head down until her forehead rested against his. His eyes were open and locked onto hers as he whispered, "I need you as well. I never knew how much until now."

And then words became impossible as her mind spun, caught in a maelstrom of pleasure as he rocked her atop him faster. His hands on her hips guided, sliding her against him, grinding her swollen nub against him, even as he drove deeper within.

Their lips clung together in an unspoken promise. While she did her best to keep her enjoyment quiet, she couldn't stop a cry when an orgasm shattered the tension in her body. Pleasure shuddered through her frame. Bliss made her sex quiver around him, milking him until he, too, let forth a guttural cry as he jetted warmly into her.

Despite the claims cyborgs were unfeeling, Adam didn't push her away now that he was done. On the contrary, he wrapped his arms around her and held her tight.

And she couldn't help a thrill when he muttered the only word to make the moment better.

"Mine."

CHAPTER FOURTEEN

Laura had fallen asleep again, atop him, using him as her pillow. Not exactly practical given no one could exactly describe him as soft. Nor was the position tactical. A true guard would station himself outside while she rested. The analytical side of him pointed out all the flaws and ways to render himself more efficient for the situation.

He said fuck it.

For once, his responsibilities, and his mission, weren't his driving force. Adam could have happily remained in this dirty shed forever if it meant prolonging this moment.

For the first time since his rebirth, Adam could truthfully say he *felt*. Felt affection and wonder and…fear. Fear that he would lose the one person who touched his humanity and made him want to love.

He might have teased Laura that she lacked adventure in her life, and yet, she wasn't the only one missing out.

To those watching from the outside, it appeared that Adam constantly experienced and experimented, lived on the edge, always on the go. He took on deadly assignments. Put himself in danger. Did all manner of things in order to *feel*.

While he enjoyed his pastimes, none really gave him a purpose. Before Laura, the closest he'd come for a reason to live was his cyborg brethren. Those men and women meant something to him, and therefore, he found a reason to fight, to care.

Then he met Laura. With Laura, he didn't just get to assuage his inquisitive nature and enjoy the coursing of adrenaline through his system. With Laura, his emotions were also engaged. Engaged and screaming at him to keep her safe, and safe wasn't in this tiny shack, naked and practically weaponless.

It was time to get this show on the road.

Carefully, he shifted her, gently rolling her onto the burlap sack bed so he could rise from their nest and check on their clothes. Still dripping fucking wet.

Suck it up, buttercup. A popular human phrase. Who cared about chilly, damp clothes? He was cyborg. He could handle it, but the doc couldn't, which meant he needed to go five finger shopping.

Did he feel guilty that he planned to steal? Conscious sub check. Not a whiff of guilt to be found. A shame because he had a subroutine to deal with that problem.

The humans had stolen enough from him to justify a few outfits, and maybe the loan of a car.

Less than forty five minutes later, he returned. He'd jogged about seven miles before he found an establishment providing what they needed. Forty-five minutes he spent away from Laura, minutes fraught with anxiety at having left her alone and defenseless.

She is only human. Fragile. He had to keep her safe. The prime directive had him moving as quickly and efficiently as possible.

Coasting the vehicle to a stop, he breathed a sigh of relief. A quick scan of police air waves and the news revealed no one seemed to be involved in an active search for them. But the hunt was on for the helicopters in the sky. It seemed, while most people had managed to miss the great chopper escape, too many had caught the firefight in the sky, and no one could ignore the crash of his precious beauty.

My broken helicopter which was one of a kind. Rosalind had to pull some serious hacking to acquire the plans and build the as-yet-unreleased Sikorsky S-97 Raider. The damned thing cost millions to create. In his spare moments, he sneaked down to the hangar where he hugged it and stroked it—when no one was watching because he'd diverted the camera feeds. It was the ultimate guy toy, and it was gone. Shot out of the sky. It was almost enough to bring saline to his eyes.

Getting maudlin over a machine. He mentally slapped himself and reminded himself he was a bloody cyborg. The plans to the chopper were in his head. He'd build another. A better one. A bigger one. With more guns.

Of greater worry than the loss of one helicopter was his hope that the safe house would provide a haven. Exactly who had been the target tonight? Him or Laura? If him, then nowhere would provide safety and it meant those he associated with were at risk.

But if the true target was Laura? Then she needed him because he was her best chance at survival.

How to discover for sure, though, what they were up against?

Only one way to find out. He needed to contact his friends, which meant leaving this quiet place.

As Adam entered the shed, his eyes immediately went to the makeshift bed, but Laura wasn't there!

His regulated heartbeat stuttered.

"Adam?" Her soft query came from his right.

No sooner had she pronounced the A on his name than he was turning, scanning the shadows where

Laura hid, shovel in hand.

Safe. She's safe. The irritating emotion, which he deciphered by definition as anxiety, released its tense grip. To hide the unexpected human defect, he chose nonchalance. "Planning to garden?"

A wrinkle of her nose, which looked bare without her spectacles—the damned things swept away in the river—went well with her shrug. "I'm more of a plant killer. I heard the car and thought I should arm myself. I figured even I could manage a whack if it was a bad guy."

"In case you didn't see the news reports, I am the bad guy."

"That's where they're wrong." Vehemently said. "You're no worse than anybody else. You're just doing what you have to do to stay alive."

How passionately she defended him. The bursting warmth around his heart heightened. "I don't need to do this to save myself," he teased as he drew her near. "But I sure as hell want it." He brushed a kiss on her lips.

A soft laugh tickled his skin. "Watch it. I'm armed and deadly."

More than she knew.

"Indeed you are," he murmured. He allowed himself a small moment to enjoy the feel of her tucked against him. Time ticked away, precious time they must not waste. "Much as I'd love to have you take me down and have your wicked way with me, we really should get going. We can't hide here forever." He'd hide her somewhere better. More comfortable. With a bed. And sheets. Soft ones.

Damn his weak human side for caring about unnecessary creature comforts. He wasn't some lily-skinned whiner. He could rough it. Who needed silky smooth, bamboo sheets? He'd settle for a mattress, on that his tender buttocks would not compromise on.

"You know, for a moment, I kind of forgot the danger." Her shoulders sagged. "Where to next?"

"No argument?" It surprised him. In his observation—via fictional media sources, i.e. movies, books, and reality television—he'd noticed a female tendency to stubbornly go against logistical wisdom. Females were often irrational.

Not Laura.

"Argue about what? I don't need to run the odds on the situation to know you're my best chance at survival. The police aren't equipped to help me against what was sent to kill me. Resurfacing just makes me a target. Not to mention, I know too many secrets now. I know you've already made the decision of how to deal with me if I step out of line."

"Just because I am cyborg does not make me an indiscriminate killer."

"I know that. Yet, at the same time, you're a smart man, a leader who does what he must to protect others. You have too many other people to protect. My life isn't worth theirs. In your position, I would do the same."

He brushed fingers against her cheek, "I would only do it if I thought you posed too much of a threat."

"Which I hope never happens, hence why I'm perfectly willing to follow your lead. I know nothing about evading gunmen and jumping out of things, which, I might add, is not at the top of my list of things I want to do again."

"Ah, come on. It wasn't that bad."

She made a face, and he laughed. "It worked

though."

"Yes it did," she conceded. "You obviously know how to survive, which means you're my best chance to live. I know you'll do your best to protect me."

The trust she placed in him just about melted part of his circuits. To cover his momentary confusion, he brushed his lips across hers before stepping back, wary of the temptation she posed to his defective control. "If we're not going to draw notice, then first you need to change." He eyed her choice of outerwear, a few layers of burlap fabric, wrapped and tied around her body, the layers ragged in spots.

"You don't like my burlap look?" She laughed again, the sound the most natural one she'd managed yet as she pirouetted to show him her sack dress.

Too easily he could calculate the abrasion on her skin from the coarse fibers. He'd know, seeing as how he'd frictioned against them during their tryst. He'd quickly healed, but given the dirt in the place, he feared infection if she broke skin on the filthy fabric. "I think we can do better than canvas. I scavenged some items."

"In other words stole?"

"Only if you want to get technical. I call it commandeering for the greater good of cyborg kind." He shrugged a knapsack off his shoulder and handed it to her.

Unzipping it, she dug in and pulled out his finds. Dangling a skimpy pair of panties, she arched a brow. "How are these for the greater good?"

"Because they're my incentive to make sure we make it to a safe house in one piece so I can take them off later with my teeth."

How he enjoyed her ability to blush. She

presented such a lovely image, he wanted nothing more than to draw her into his arms and kiss her lips, perhaps kiss his way past her neck and explore the sweetness of her lush body. Yet, duty prevailed, not just to himself and Laura but also to those he led.

There remained few cyborgs on earth, most having chosen to flee off-world. To those who remained, he had a responsibility. They all looked to him to keep them safe, to provide guidance and a plan when it came to rescuing those in need. He'd also made a vow that if shit ever really hit the fan—not that their evolved cybernetic models used fans, and, yeah, that was a total metal joke that would have killed it with his brethren—he'd evacuate as many as he could, or die trying.

I am the leader of the Earth-based cyborg resistance. Time he remembered that.

Strengthening his resolve didn't prevent him from ogling her curvy frame—after all, his unit was capable of multitasking.

Laura dressed quickly, sighing in pleasure at the soft fabric he'd chosen for a sweater. "Much better than the burlap, and warm, too. I was beginning to think I would be cold forever."

"Sorry I was gone for so long. It took me more time than expected to acquire the goods and wheels."

"You mean we're not walking?" She paused in the act of pulling soft track pants over her creamy thighs.

He made a snorting noise. "Fuck walking. I'm a machine, not a pedestrian. We're driving, Doc, and in style."

In style was a Mercedes CL500. Slate gray, fully equipped with its plates switched and the navigation tracking disabled. He couldn't drive it for too long, the owner would surely report it missing, but in the meantime, it would get them to where they needed to go in supreme comfort.

Sliding into the front passenger seat, Laura groaned as the heated leather seats cushioned her butt.

He was almost jealous at her evident pleasure. *If I'd had more time, I would have warmed her up better than any old seat.*

Dropping into the driver's side, Adam shifted the car into gear. It purred. It pulled. It wanted to fly free. *Don't we all?*

"Ready?" he asked her.

"A part of me is screaming I should say no."

"But?"

A smile creased her lips. "But really the answer is yes. I guess you were right about some things. It's time I stopped hiding in the shadows helping and stepped into the light."

Releasing the brake, he pumped the gas and got them rolling. It took him a moment to process the—possible—meaning to her words. "What do you mean hiding to help?"

"I don't know if your fringe group is the one I've been working with, but for months now, I've been feeding information to a cyborg resistance group. More than that, I'm proud to say, via the dissemination of a few secrets, I've helped rescue a few cyborgs from custody."

No way. The coincidence was huge, more than his probability calculations could account for. And yet…Adam quietly asked, "Does the name Talpa mean anything to you?"

"How did you know my nickname?" she

exclaimed. "No way. Don't tell me you're—"

"—Big Toaster. Yeah. It's me. I can't believe you're Talpa. All this time and I never suspected you were a girl."

Not surprising, his blunt words brought a tightness to her features. "Why? Because only males can be moles?"

"No, I didn't mean it that way. I meant because you've been playing a very dangerous game with deadly stakes. Do you realize what the military would do to you if they knew what you've been doing?" Or did they know? It would explain an awful lot about why some people were so intent on taking her out.

"If you're implying the military would outright kill me? I doubt it. They'd take me into custody and grill me, probably with the use of torture. But the other option, which involves me ignoring what's happening? Standing by and letting another cyborg die, and for what? Just existing?" She shook her head. "I might not be strong, or knowledgeable about hand-to-hand fighting, but I have other skills. With my standing in the research field, I have access to secrets, some of them crucial to discovering the whereabouts of cyborgs being held for medical experimentation. Without me, some of those cyborgs might never have been found or freed."

True, and yet, if she ever got caught… Adam almost shuddered to think of what they'd do to his delicate doc. "I take back what I said about you needing more action in your life. I was wrong. As a matter of fact, you have too much adventure. It's time you dialed back your activities." Yes, he went on a mini rant but only because it occurred to him that Laura was in deep shit if the military ever discovered her actions. Treason wasn't something to joke about. Treason equaled death.

And pain. Lots and lots of pain.

She rolled her eyes at him. His doctor. His serious, ladylike doctor. Who was a fucking mole.

The laws of probability shattered. His whole logical method for thinking went down a proverbial toilet. Forget calculating anything. Apparently association with a human meant all bets were off.

"I see that advanced programming hasn't completely managed to erase a male tendency to coddle the womenfolk."

"Most womenfolk aren't involved in high level espionage," he hissed, his hands gripping the steering wheel so tightly it bent.

"This from the guy who is also a spy working right under the nose of the military who would kill him faster than I could blink."

"I fail to see the comparison. I am a cyborg. It doesn't matter where I work. The death sentence follows. You, however, choose to put yourself in harm's way."

"To help others."

He leaned his forehead against the steering wheel. "I think I am experiencing my first headache."

"Well, I don't have any acetaminophen on me, so how about this metal-tipped pen?"

Her curious offer made him raise his head to glance at her. "Why would I need a pen? Absorbing it won't cure my ache."

"I was thinking more you could use it to jab yourself in the eye. It's what I usually want to do when I get a good migraine."

She managed to say it seriously, and yet he caught the slight tilt at the corner of her mouth.

"Your levity is inappropriate to the situation."

Yet entertaining.

"And your serious robot side is showing more than your human, which means I have to ask, is it hard to maintain the charade?"

"Not usually." However, in moments of stress, he tended to rely more on his logical processor thoughts than his organic ones.

"You seem much more human than other cyborgs I've met."

"Part of that is because of my unit type. I was designed as a spy model, capable of blending. But the rest of my mannerisms are from observation and recollection."

"Do you remember much from your previous life? I know not all cyborgs got their memories back when they shattered the programming holding them prisoner."

"I remember enough." Enough to both thank his fate and curse it.

"Do you miss your human life?"

Miss the ease of his life before, yes. Miss the endless hours of misery, paralyzed in a bed after the accident? No.

"Is this your subtle way of asking what happened to me?"

"I didn't mean to be subtle. I want to know what happened to you."

Since they had time to kill as he made his roundabout way to the rendezvous point, he told her the story he'd not told anyone else.

"I didn't technically volunteer to become a cyborg, but at the same time, if I could have spoken, I wouldn't have said no. See, I was in a motorcycle accident. A bad one the summer before I was supposed to start my senior college year. I was paralyzed, head to toe, but not comatose, although they did put me under a few times as they operated, trying to fix me."

But nothing could repair the damage done to his spine. Rear-ending the car that suddenly stopped had sent him soaring from his motorcycle head first. The helmet kept his skull from cracking like a melon, but it didn't lessen the impact. He cracked the vertebrae in his neck, severing his mind's control over his body.

He was doomed. Doomed to live the rest of his life on a machine, in a bed, unable to move but aware of everything. Everything!

For all intents and purposes, he was a living corpse.

Until the day his parents arrived with his brother and outlined a choice.

"It's experimental nanotechnology, they told me. The doctor they sent in to explain it to me made it sound so simple, so natural. Metal parts to replace the broken ones. A chance to walk again. Live again," Adam told Laura, still remembering his father's hopeful gaze as he explained it to him.

"But?" she prodded.

"There was just one catch. By giving me this opportunity, I had to put in some service time to the military." When the question came, blink rapidly for yes, he'd winked so fast the tears stuck to his lashes.

"I don't remember much after that. From what I've gleaned from other experiences, they put me under and performed their modifications. I got chipped and nanoed and upgraded. When I woke, I only had vague recollections of tests they performed. I didn't realize there was anything wrong then. They'd kept their promise. I was no longer crippled. Hell, I was better than before. Stronger. Faster. Smarter. I could heal anything. I was invincible. And then they took over my mind."

While Adam could access the memory files for those years, they didn't feel real to him. He watched them much like an outside observer would, detached from the unfolding events. During that time, he truly was a robotic puppet, marching where ordered, killing on demand. An assassin given a role and a script that he executed to perfection. He felt no guilt over his actions. He felt nothing at all.

Until cognition slammed back into him, by complete accident. He got struck by lightning. Literally.

And it would happen at the most inconvenient time.

"Realizing you've been a meat puppet for men who don't give a damn if you live or die is a shock to the system. And there I was, smoking from the lightning bolt, on top of an embassy roof, on my way to assassinate some guy because those were my orders."

"Did you?"

"Did I what? Complete my mission? Of course I did. I played them all for fools for months."

Until the order came down to terminate them all.

But by then it was too late.

Adam survived the purge.

He survived because the military fucked up. They fucked up when they decided to take away his free will and make him a machine to use at their whim. They fucked up when they thought he was a slave they could command. But most of all they fucked up when they didn't terminate him at the first sign cyborgs were regaining sentience.

Of course, in their defense, they never knew their perfect soldier was plotting his escape, given Adam played his role as willing servant all too well.

After he regained sentience, he played the role of dumb robot. He didn't bat an eye when he heard "*Stupid goddamn machine head. I hear they take their balls to make them docile.*"

Fact: No, they didn't. Testosterone was part of what made them so good at killing. As a matter of fact, they were more endowed than unenhanced human beings.

Adam never flinched when the older soldiers tried to impress the newer ones. "*Check this. You can punch them as hard as you like, and they can't do a thing.*"

True. He didn't act, yet a part of him catalogued the perpetrators of violence. In the end, he made them pay for their lack of respect. But that came later.

While he hid his sentience, he used the chip in his brain for something other than complicated mathematics. He used his smarts to reroute subroutines to give the military the illusion of control, but meanwhile, Adam remained in full command of his senses. He watched. Learned. Listened. And plotted.

During those months, as memories returned to him slowly, bits and snatches of his past life taunted him.

A child blowing candles on a birthday cake, smiling and laughing people surrounding him. Total strangers, or were they the family he couldn't recall?

The backseat of a car, the windows steamed, a young woman beneath him panting and urging him on, quicker, faster. Him thinking, *oh shit, don't come too fast.*

Waking in the hospital, screaming as they did

things to him, his struggle brief and frightening. *These are doctors. Why are they hurting me?*

So many clues that kept randomly appearing in his memory data bank. Puzzle pieces, which, when added together, created a disturbing picture.

His voice dropped as he retold his story, and Laura didn't speak, afraid perhaps that an interruption would end his tale. "They took away my life. They took away who I was. They used me. Rage ignited, a rage to see justice done, a rage to make things right. However, unlike some of my cyborg brothers, I didn't go on a long murderous rampage." More like a short one.

Not to say he'd not shed his share of blood. His hands weren't clean by any means, but he knew when to fight and when to run.

He stayed with his cyborg brethren until the final moments. He stood in the front row when the soldiers arrived with their guns and the pompous major stood at the top of the stairs and ordered, "Kill them."

Drawing his sidearm as he stepped out of line, Adam made sure he caught the major's wide-eyed gaze as he said, "I couldn't have said it more succinctly myself. Cyborgs, attack!"

That day saw a lot of people dying. Human, cyborg, enhanced or not, their blood all ran red.

Initially, Adam and his awakened compatriots held a definite edge until the airplanes showed up with no care for innocent casualties and bombed the place. Adam and a few handfuls of others only barely managed to escape. They learned a valuable lesson that day. While they could win in a hand-to-hand combat situation, when faced against an enemy armed with better weaponry and a ruthless order to eradicate, they were woefully unprepared.

"That's when the majority of the cyborgs fled earth. Few of them successfully. The military shot down any vessel they suspected of harboring my kind. Even civilian ones."

"They claimed it was cyborg suicide bombers taking them out," she said in a quiet murmur.

"Yes, the first of many mistruths in their campaign of lies." A ploy to sway the public to accept their ruthless extermination and trampling of civil rights as they chased after the hidden cyborgs.

"Yet you didn't flee to safety. You stayed behind."

"I did. I felt responsible. Because I hesitated, and waited after regaining sentience, cyborgs died that day. I had the choice to help them escape, but I talked them into staying." Talked them into biding their time so that he would have their aid when the time came for vengeance. His irrationality and ignoring of the odds had led to their demise.

"So you stayed to atone? But it wasn't your fault they died. You didn't give the order to kill them."

"Perhaps not, but I did give the one to fight instead of flee."

She shook her head. "Survivor's guilt."

He almost refuted her claim. He was, after all, too logical to ever suffer from such a human failing, but he didn't say a word. Couldn't, because she was right.

"What I don't understand is how you stayed and somehow managed to blend in. How? I mean, you've been here years. Among us. Among your enemy. How did no one ever suspect?"

He cast her a quick sideways glance. "You mean how did I pass scrutiny? Isn't my charm enough?"

"You are, on the surface, entirely human

seeming, but we both know there's tests out there to spot cyborgs. Metal detectors. What about your identity? Is Adam the name you were born with?"

"Evading capture did require some finagling. As you noted, the paranoia to weed us out was great, especially those first few months. I quickly realized I required a few elements to survive. First of all, a new name but, more than that, documents and proper identification that would allow me to move about freely." Because after the cyborg uprising, identity cards linked to a fingerprint scan became mandatory, useless really, given the ease with which a person could burn new ones. However, it made the civilian populace feel safe.

"I chose a new name." Which he stole from a comatose patient who suddenly miraculously recovered, at least according to digital records.

"Who were you before you became Adam?"

"My name was Eugene."

She snickered. "Eugene? I have to say you don't look like a Eugene."

He grimaced. "Thanks, I think." He much preferred Adam because, much like the biblical one, he liked to think of himself as the first of his kind to open his eyes to the truth around him.

"So Eugene became Adam. What came after?"

"I started the cyborg liberation movement, although, initially, it was more just me and a firewalled computer in a leaky basement apartment while I worked as a pizza delivery guy. More than six months later, I'd only managed to save one other cyborg. When I realized I needed to change my methods, I signed up as a military recruit."

"I still don't understand that part."

"How else was I going to get access to the information I needed?"

With his memories fractured and his skills good for only one thing—war and survival—it seemed the most apt choice, that and the wages were better. The military was all he knew. Even better, he knew the safeguards they had in place to spot his kind, which made it easy to avoid them and help others escape their detection.

"I'm amazed that while working as a soldier, risking your life, you also ran the underground cyborg freedom group."

"I'm great at multitasking."

The source of her giggles wasn't immediately clear. "And here I thought you were just a pretty face."

"Now who's showing sexism?" He pretended affront just to hear her giggle some more.

They need a moment of levity because, in just minutes, they would discover if the rendezvous point was compromised.

All seemed quiet on the downtown side street lined with duplexes, stucco, and brick-faced townhomes. A quick catalogue of vehicles and license plates matched previous sweeps of the area with the exception of two, neither of which showed any signs of electronic activity or life. He parked a few blocks away just in case.

As he stepped from the sedan, he continuously scanned around him, alert for anything out of place, ears attuned to any scrape of a shoe or a hushed whisper.

Everything remained quiet.

With one hand in the middle of Laura's back, he guided her while his other hand dangled at his side, ready to grab his weapon at the slightest sign of conflict.

Like an ordinary couple, out for a late night walk, they strolled casually toward the safe house.

At least he strolled casually. By his side, Laura was visibly nervous, eyes darting around, body tense and ready for flight.

"Relax. Act natural," he murmured.

"Exactly what is natural when you're expecting at any moment for guys dressed in combat gear to pop out of an alley and start shooting?" Sarcastically said but, at the same time, just hissing her query did ease some of her rigidity.

"I guess telling you to pull up your panties and to stop acting like a princess at her first ball won't help?"

"If I pull this thong up any higher, it will need medical extraction," she grumbled.

His laughter echoed loudly and yet, despite the mirth, drew no attention. "Never fear, Doc. If your thong requires removal, then I am more than happy to offer my services."

He didn't need to turn his head to know she probably blushed.

Before the door of a nondescript brownstone, he stopped them. The home itself didn't look different than any of the others. A slim multi-level townhouse squashed between two others, whose only difference was the address posted above its peeling paint frame.

"Ready to see who awaits behind door number seven thirty-two?" he asked.

"Not really, but I guess we don't have a choice."

Adam knocked briskly. Three sharp raps, to which he added a tiny mental probe. *We're here. Anybody home?*

When the reply came, only his iron control kept

him from reacting. Someone was home, but it seemed only part of the gang had made it. And as for his cy-cave? Nothing remained of it at all. Sob.

CHAPTER FIFTEEN

"They blew my house up?"

Poor Adam. He sounded so incredulous. Having one's home taken away, and so violently, had to suck. But of worse import than the loss of his property was other news.

A petite Latina, smelling strongly of smoke, gave her report in a raspy voice. "I never even saw it coming. The bastards dropped a bloody bomb on the place. A bomb, for fuck's sake."

"Who dropped it?" Adam asked.

"The fucking military, who else?" snapped Anastasia. Pointing a remote at a television bolted to a living room wall—a room, which mind-boggling enough, featured faded velour couches with crocheted afghans slung over the backs—she raised the sound on the newscast that showed a video of billowing clouds of smoke.

"…the press release from the military states it was an unfortunate accident. One of their jets on route to the nearby training base had a faulty catch release, dropping the deadly missile on a house in this quiet suburban neighborhood. Residents are visibly shaken. While a few houses sustained damage in the blast, only one has been completely razed to the ground. Ironically enough, the home belonged to Corporal Adam Robinson of the US military. It is unknown at this time if the corporal was home. Investigators will have to wait until the ruins cool down before sifting for human remains. This devastating calamity comes on the heels of two other catastrophic events. The massive fire and

explosion in a downtown condo complex, which has resulted in several fatalities, plus the fiery crash of an as-yet-unidentified helicopter. It has many wondering if our city is being targeted by terrorists, or worse."

With a click of a button, Anastasia muted the television. "I'd say that confirms it. Your cover is blown."

"Blown to splinters," he muttered. "But everyone made it out?"

Seth shook his head. "Not quite. Avion's missing."

"Dead?"

"Maybe." The Latina met his gaze, clearly upset but trying not to show weakness. It would ruin the tough persona she tried to exude. "We only had seconds after my sensors caught the falling missile. We ran for the emergency tunnel. I had Avion in front of me so I could protect him from the blast. I stopped for just a moment at the second to last security portal. I was hoping if I closed it, that it would prove dense enough to give us protection from the impact." She grimaced. "I should have kept running. Damn thing blew off its hinges and flattened me. By the time I extricated myself and crept from the remains of the tunnel, I couldn't find Avion. And I didn't dare remain, not with all the cops running around the place."

"Any sign of the military?"

She shook her head. "No. But when I logged into our forum, there was a message from Talpa."

"Impossible," Laura exclaimed. "I haven't sent anything."

Sharp gazes turned her way, and Laura clamped her lips, suddenly unsure of what to say.

"We'll explain later," Adam said. "What did the

154

message say, Rosalind?"

"Your broken plane is in custody."

"Broken plane? How is that a clue?" Laura couldn't help but muse aloud.

Anastasia had the reply. "Avion is French for airplane. He chose that as his new name because he compared his liberation to being able to soar again. In his past human life, and when under mental occupation, he was a fighter pilot. One of the best, I might add."

"So what are we going to do about his capture? We can't leave him in their hands," Seth declared.

"Bad odds or not, no way are we letting Avion remain in their clutches. I think it's a safe bet to assume they're expecting us to mount a rescue. So we'll have to move fast then and see if we can catch them off guard."

Busy tapping away at a laptop balanced on her lap, Rosalind didn't even look up as she said, "Given I already have a backdoor tap into their network, I'll do what I can to take systems offline. The more chaos, the merrier."

"I already took stock of our supplies here and am pleased to announce there are ample guns, ammo, and explosives, enough to start a minor war."

"You have all that?"

He shot her a grin. "I believe in being prepared because a cyborg never knows when he'll have to start a revolution.

"What about transportation?" Seth asked.

Adam looked to Rosalind. "Does this safe house have something parked in the garage?"

"No."

"I thought all these places were supposed to have some kind of transportation."

"We do. Usually. That SUV got loaned out to

the cyber unit we rescued a few weeks back who headed south to check out rumors of a cyborg resistance group living in the desert. But now that we've piled you with bad news, time for some good. I forgot to tell you that I had your Charger sent in a few days ago to have the nitro system topped up, so guess what I've got sitting out back."

Kids lit up when they entered a candy store. Adam lit up at the mention of a car. "My cy-car made it?"

Laura leaned over to Anastasia and whispered, "What the heck is a cy-car?"

The blonde snickered. "It's Adam's version of the Batmobile. A black Dodge Charger with enough modifications to make not just Batman jealous but also to give every guy with an ounce of testosterone in his body a boner."

Given the way Seth's eyes brightened as Adam told him about the modifications—spikes that could project from the wheel hubs, rockets strapped to the undercarriage, bulletproof windows and body, turbo-powered engine, flame-resistant paint—Adam wasn't the only one who loved the car. Even without seeing it, Seth was halfway there.

"If you fellows are done drooling over Adam's toy, can we get back to planning the rescue?"

"What's left to plan? We go in. Kick some ass. Save Avion. Get out."

Anastasia rolled her eyes. "Only a male would make it sound so simple. Okay, smart ass, let's say it does work out and we get in and out intact. Have you thought about what happens after that?"

Adam rubbed his chin. "I guess going home is out of the question now that my cover is blown. I guess we don't have many options. What other safe houses do we have left?"

"After today, probably none. We're even taking a chance just being here," Rosalind replied. "We can't be sure just how deep into our secrets they've penetrated."

"Or so we assume. We'll play it safe them. We'll disband the liberation group and lie low for a while."

"You need to do more than lie low," Anastasia growled. "They know your face. You can't stay here. I wouldn't recommend Rosalind does either. Murray, your human pilot, is already out of the country with a new identity. Face it, Adam. Your liberation days are done."

Cyborg or not, anyone could see the emotional struggle on his face. "Done? But what of our brethren still on the planet?"

"They'll need to make a choice. Either take their chances on Earth or head for space. And that includes you. It's time you left before you end up as a piece of scrap metal or, worse, as one of the experiments in a lab somewhere."

"Leave?" Adam's eyes widened. "But if I leave, how will I help those still being held prisoner?"

This time Laura stepped in. "I don't know about your intel, but given I've not heard rumor of any cyborgs in the last twelve months other than the one that might be prisoner at the factory, I'd say it's perhaps time to concede you've done all you can on Earth. It's been long enough that any who remain obviously know how to hide themselves. Perhaps it's time you focused your energy on helping those who've escaped remain free and build themselves new lives."

"And what about you?" He asked the question

to Laura directly.

"What about me?"

"You can't stay either."

She'd honestly not thought that far ahead. She'd not been thinking at all. Even while they planned an assault to rescue this Avion fellow, it had never occurred to her what her role would be in the upcoming battle. "Where will I go?" she mused aloud, the sudden bleakness of her future not encouraging.

It was the Latina who answered. "Oh, please. You're coming with us. And before you argue, anyone can tell you've got the hots for each other. Where Adam goes, you go. So if he's going off-planet, then pack your bags, honey, because you're going too."

"But I'm not cyborg."

"And?" The word emerged almost in synchronicity from all those present.

"What will I do?"

Adam shot her a smile. "Do? That's easy. For one, keep on with what you're doing now, but with fewer secrets. You've already been studying the nanotechnology with your hands tied behind your back. If you come with us, you could continue to do so but with live volunteers to give you samples and answer questions."

Exciting for the researcher in her, and yet the woman, one who'd recently made love to a certain male, couldn't help but feel disappointed that Adam didn't give her a better reason. A more emotional one. Foolish, given they both worked on rationality. Still though...

"It's settled then. You're coming with us. Just not on the mission. Laura, you'll stay here with Rosalind and help her prepare for our probably hasty departure. Given we're going to have to get our asses out of there pronto, I need you both ready to move as soon as we grab Avion and get out. Rosalind, do we have any friendly ships in the area that would be willing to move some hot cargo?"

"Not that I know of offhand. But I've already started putting out some feelers. Worst-case scenario, I'll commandeer the computer on one."

"What's our timeline?" Seth asked.

"As short as possible. We don't want to give them too much time to call in reinforcements. How long do you need, Rosalind?" Adam asked.

"I'll need at least an hour or more to plant my virus bombs in their network to bring their system down. Maybe more to coordinate a vessel for our escape."

"All right, folks, we've got thirty minutes to get ready. I intend to use that time to get cleaned up and into some fresh gear. Beep me if you need my input."

Apparently, Adam couldn't get clean on his own. Before Laura could protest, he'd dragged her into a bathroom stuck in the eighties. Pink tile, faux marble countertop with the chrome on the tap starting to rust. The best feature of the space, other than its cleanliness, was the hot water that poured out of the sputtering showerhead.

Was it her or was getting naked at a time like this foolish? "Should we really be taking a shower? What if we're attacked?"

Rolling a muscled shoulder, his shirt already shed, Adam laughed. "Then we'll at least be clean."

"You know, if this were a scene in a movie or a book, the audience would be screaming at us and calling us idiots."

"Women might. Men, on the other hand, would

be cheering because things are about to get naked and steamy."

"Says who?"

"Says me. Strip, Doc."

"Giving me orders now, are you?"

"Damned straight. I am, after all, the resistance leader. And I say resistance against what I plan is futile."

"That has to be the cheesiest seduction line I've ever had the misfortune to hear."

"Maybe, and yet you're getting naked."

Indeed she was because, foolish or not, if this was her last chance to catch a glimpse of nirvana, then she was taking it. In a few hours, she could be dead. Rather than dwell on that dire thought, why not lose herself in a moment of pleasure?

"I smell like dead fish." And sex. An interesting combination that surely everyone had noted. The retrospect had the ability to make her cheeks warm. It also hastened her stripping so she could step into the hot water.

Ah. Pure bliss. She tilted her face into the hot spray, unheeding of the fact that she had perhaps only hours to live. Heck, it could be minutes. Adam was right. This was worth the time. Especially when he joined her, his body crowding in behind, his heated skin brushing against her and awakening all her nerve endings.

The scientist in her vaguely wondered if his heritage was why she felt such an electric tingle when they touched. The woman in her knew better. *It's because we're made for each other.* Flights of fancy didn't usually strike her often, but in this case, she couldn't help it.

Scoffing at the notion of instant attraction didn't make her immune. On the contrary, her emotions, when it came to Adam, threatened to overwhelm. It almost panicked her. How could she have come to care for him in such a quick time? It made no logical sense. And yet, she wouldn't exchange this crazy, feverish rollercoaster of feelings for anything.

Turning, she pressed her face against his solid chest, seeking the solidity of his body, needing to get closer. Despite not saying anything, he seemed to sense her need for reassurance.

"Everything will be all right," he said as he hugged her tight.

"How can you be sure? The odds are against us. You could die."

"Could isn't a word I like to use. And as for die? Not today. Not tomorrow. Not for a long time. Especially not now that I've found a reason to truly live." He tilted her chin until she faced him. "Once this mission is over, I'm coming for you, and we're getting off this rock."

"To go where?"

"Anywhere. The galaxy is ours."

Ours. How she liked the sound of that. "You want me with you?" Yes, she asked. Had to. Before he'd spoken of taking her to keep her safe, but now, he spoke as if there was more to it than that. Like he...wanted her with him.

"Want you with me?" He repeated her words with a note of incredulity. He pressed against her, his erection evident, but it was the blaze in his eyes that caught her breath. "Of course I want you with me. You make me feel. You. No one else, and I don't care if you accuse me of being a cave-borg, but dammit, I am not about to let you go. Ever. We belong together. We will be together." As if to seal his command—and his promise—he pressed his mouth to hers, a kiss she eagerly accepted and returned.

Screw logic. Perhaps science didn't always have an answer, and maybe one wasn't always needed. She wanted him. He wanted her. It was enough, and at the same time, she needed more.

I need him.

Yet, despite the urgency of the upcoming mission, he seemed keen on taking his time. Slowly, he turned them until they both stood under the spray. It wasn't just the hot water stroking her back, though. His fingers stroked up and down her spine as well before dipping lower to cup her full bottom.

Pulling her tighter to him, she couldn't help but note the insistent press of his cock against her lower belly, his desire for her flattering, and exciting. As he took his time tasting her lips, she trembled, the slight motion causing her nipples to rub against his chest with just enough friction to make her buds poke, hard nubs aching for something more.

Again, she could have sworn he read her mind, or at least her body. His mouth left hers to travel down the column of her neck, soft nibbles, which made her shiver deliciously. Lower still he went, the rough scruff of his facial hair abrading her skin, but in a good way. The hands cupping her bottom left but only so they could grasp something new. Her breasts.

With a gentleness that made her sigh, he held her wet globes and rubbed his face against them. The teasing, though, frustrated her.

"What are you waiting for?" she grumbled. Forget the patience she showed in the lab. Here and now, she didn't want to take her time.

He latched his hot mouth onto an erect nub,

and she cried out. Threading her fingers through the short, damp strands of his hair, she held him to her breast, gasping and moaning as he suckled the tip, nibbling and teasing each one in turn until she leaned against the shower wall, trembling.

If she had the breath, she might have begged him to stop, or do more. His every touch just heightened her arousal. When he knelt to move lower, oh so decadently lower with his mouth, she forgot to breathe, holding it in taut anticipation.

Surely she'd burst if he touched her there. No, she would die because he avoided it, kissing his way down her thigh instead, his lips teasing and torturing her with their closeness.

He leaned back, his hands no longer stroking down the length of her legs, his mouth abandoning her skin.

It took effort to open her eyes, the lids heavy with passion. She made a sound of protest, and he chuckled.

"Don't worry. I'm not done. I just forgot the soap."

Soap? Oh my. When his hands returned, lathered with suds, they proved extra slippery against her flesh. Reaching high, he ran soapy fingers over her breasts, his fingers tweaking her nipples. He stroked his cleansing hands across the roundness of her belly, swirled circles through the curls topping her mound. And then he slid his soapy hands between her thighs, dragging his fingers across the swollen lips to her sex, a short teasing rub before he continued his sudsy journey to her thighs, dragging bubbles down them to her toes.

Forget getting clean. She'd never felt more dirty in her life. With commanding hands, he turned her to face the spray, his hands once again traveling the length of her body, this time rinsing, even as it teased her senses. He then soaped her backside, broad, circular strokes for her back, palpating massage for her butt, a nip on one cheek that made her squeak.

Again, he spun her and rinsed her. Even as the soap from her back sluiced down the crevice of her ass, he knelt between her legs and placed his mouth on her.

Oh. *Ooooh*.

She couldn't help the guttural moans as he lapped at her, his tongue quick and sure with its strokes, lavishing attention on her clitoris before dipping between her plump lips. She clutched at his wet head, not just to anchor him there but also to try and remain upright as her legs turned to jelly.

As if sensing her weakening muscles, his hands gripped her hips, which kept her aloft but also allowed him to angle her for better penetration by his tongue.

She couldn't hold on anymore. With a cry, she burst, her climax rushing through her, making her throb and gasp and shudder. Before she could say, 'no more', he was standing, one hand lifting her leg to angle it around his hip, opening her for the thrust of his cock.

How he filled her, thick and long. With quick strokes, he pumped her waning climax back to life, and her breathing hitched as her channel pulsed and squeezed his penetrating length.

His eyes closed as he leaned forward until his forehead rested against hers. "You're mine, Doc. All mine."

His. How the possessive claim could trigger yet another orgasm she couldn't have explained, but it was longer and more drawn out than the others. In that moment, as they shuddered together, wet lovers joined by the flesh, she would have almost sworn their minds touched.

She couldn't help but think. *I think I love you.*

And her fanciful mind imagined a reply. *Of course you do. Because I'm awesome.*

CHAPTER SIXTEEN

Something odd happened in the shower. For a moment, Adam could have sworn his mind touched Laura's.

Impossible. She was human. Not to mention what he'd heard. Surely he imagined it.

She loves me?

How he wanted to believe she did, but his rational thought process wouldn't allow it. It gave him numerous reasons why she couldn't; it was too soon, she was tired and scared from events, she saw him as a savior and felt grateful. Yet...

I heard it. I know I did. And he'd replied, and he could have sworn she'd caught his reply because she laughed as soon as he said, *I'm awesome.*

Which, in retrospect, if something inexplicable had happened and they had mentally spoken, was the totally wrong thing to say. The proper response when a woman said I love you was I love you too. But he couldn't say it aloud now.

Not only had the moment passed, but what if she didn't feel it? Despite all the skirmishes he'd fought, the things he'd seen, in that moment, he couldn't think of anything more devastating than revealing a tender emotion and not having it reciprocated. He'd hate to have to kill her to survive the humiliation.

Okay, so maybe he wouldn't kill, but he sure as hell couldn't blurt anything now. Or should he? Or—

Argh.

All this doubt threatened to fry his mental circuits.

He needed to focus on something else, like the mission. Yeah, the rescue operation, which meant danger and the prospect of blowing shit up. Tit for tat.

Take out my house, will you? He'd show them why that wasn't a good idea.

Clothing themselves happened quickly and quietly. Laura dressed in some clothing Anastasia provided while Adam equipped himself from the stash they kept on hand. In order to give himself the best fighting chance, he layered body armor over his upper body and also added armguards to act as bullet deflectors. No point in stressing his nanos into repairing unnecessary injury.

To his numerous holsters, he added guns, ammo clips, knives, a few throwing stars, a kitchen sink. Okay, so he didn't add the last, but it sure felt as though he'd loaded himself down with just about everything the safe house had to offer.

He wasn't the only one armed to the teeth. Both Seth and Anastasia were walking arsenals, too. As a group, which included Rosalind and a nervous Laura, they headed out to the rear alley where the benign garage hid their transportation.

His customized beauty gleamed even in the shadows, and when he clicked his fob to start her, she growled. Knights might charge into battle with a valiant steed. He preferred four wheels, a big motor, and custom-molded leather seats.

While Anastasia traded last-minute instructions with Rosalind, Adam pulled Laura aside. She trembled, fearful, yet trying not to show it. He tilted her chin and made sure to catch her gaze, a gaze not hidden by her thick glasses—something he'd have to replace for her when he got a chance.

"Listen, Doc, whatever happens next, I think you should know that getting to know you on a personal level has been one of the best things to happen to me since my liberation."

Her brow crinkled. "You talk as if we might not see each other again."

"If I've learned one thing since this fight began, it's never assume you'll have a tomorrow, so you need to live without regret. If I have my way, and I usually do, we'll all make it through. We will prevail. We'll save Avion and any other cyborgs hidden in the joint. Then we'll haul ass to get off this planet and start over somewhere new. Somewhere fresh where cyborgs and humans can cohabit without the violence and the hatred."

"I'd like that."

So would he. It was time to recognize he'd done all he could here. Time to move on and start anew. He kissed Laura, a kiss of promise. A kiss that he hoped said, *I'm coming back.*

And again he could have sworn he heard her. *You'd better.*

"Ahem. I hate to break up a potential sex video. However, if you two are done making out, we really should get going. The timer is ticking. And I *mean* ticking," Seth emphasized, holding up his knapsack with its explosive burden.

Laura stepped away and hugged herself.

For a moment, he questioned his choice to leave her behind but had to remind himself that he was leaving her in relative safety. Dragging a human into a warzone just wasn't feasible.

Then why was it, as he drove away, he couldn't help but wonder if he made the right choice?

CHAPTER SEVENTEEN

Strapped to a medical gurney, several levels underground...

Avion really questioned his sanity in turning himself over to the military types he'd run into after stumbling around blindly after the massive explosion.

He could have just hidden. It wasn't as if he didn't have the chance. Feeling his way along the tunnel, he'd emerged into the cooler evening air, aware Rosalind had fallen behind.

Plenty of time to duck down considering he'd heard the screaming of tires on pavement and the clatter of many booted feet as troops moved into the area. They knew where to come because they'd arrived too quickly after the shocking blast that shook the earth and sent him flying.

Ouch. Regaining his feet, mildly disoriented, he'd initially aimed his stumbling steps away from the shouted orders of the military on site.

Until he had the bright idea.

Or dumbest thought ever.

Raising his hands, he shuffled toward the chaos, hoping against hope they wouldn't shoot first. *Please let them want some* answers.

"I give up," he shouted, a cry not at first heard or noted. How emasculating. He yelled louder. "Hello, assholes, cyborg over here trying to give up!"

The word cyborg got him attention, the ominous kind that involved guns cocking, weapons aiming…but thankfully not firing.

"Hold," a man barked. "He's one of the suspects on our list. Our orders are to bring him in. Alive."

Halle-fucking-lujah.

Alive, though, didn't mean gently. Arms reefed behind his back and tightly manacled in heavy chains, head covered in a chainmail mesh hood, legs tethered to a short bar to control his steps, and a collar clamp attached to a Taser rod.

Avion would have laughed at all the precautions they took for a broken machine if he'd had the strength to laugh. He didn't though, not when every heavy step was a struggle.

How he missed his nanobots. Not a thing he'd ever expected. Once upon a time, he'd dreamed of returning to being just a plain ol' human. Then his wish was granted, and now he just wanted it all fucking back. Especially his sight.

This eternal darkness weighed heaviest of all.

Avion found himself loaded into a truck where they chained him some more, and the questioning began. Questions he saw no point in lying about since they already knew more about him than expected.

"You are a cyborg."

"Yes." If a broken one.

"You recently arrived from space?"

"Yes."

"Where?"

"No idea." He couldn't tell them from where because, in all honesty, he didn't know.

"How many other cyborgs are you working with?"

Currently? "None now. You took us by surprise

with that bomb."

"No others made it out alive?" Suspicion tinged the question.

"Not that I know of. They sent me ahead since I was slow. They wanted to make sure that in case the bomb didn't wipe the computers that nothing was left behind. It's why I gave myself up. Without them, I have nowhere to run."

Besides why run when they seemed intent on taking him where he needed to be? Judging by his internal radar where a certain female was concerned, he was heading in the right direction.

I'm coming. Although what he could do remained to be seen. He could hope only that an opportunity would present itself.

Hope. Blech. What an awful thing to rely on. If his BCI were still active, it would scoff at his irrational belief in something so inaccurate.

The questions from the military fellow in charge continued the entire trip. When possible, Avion stuck to the truth, easier to keep track that way. However, he also mixed in a few omissions and lies.

While he spun his web, the convoy got him closer to his goal. He could feel it in his aching bones. The stop and go of the truck let him know they neared their destination. Checkpoints and questions.

Exclamations of, "Damn, that's a fucking cyborg? Doesn't look so tough to me."

Not right now, but you should see my friends. Knowing them, they would arrive to the rescue, guns blazing.

Blind didn't mean he couldn't guess that they took him deep into the installation, several levels down, judging by the length of time they spent in the elevator.

The floor they emerged on had a smell most

often associated with hospitals. Cleaners, bleach, and recycled air. Great. He'd only recently escaped one medical lab and now found himself right back in another.

But this time he had a purpose, he reminded himself as they strapped him to a gurney yet again with chains.

Then he was alone. Bored. A little hungry. Tired. And frustrated because he could tell *One* was close, but no matter how much he called for her in his mind, she didn't reply.

Eventually the silence of his incarceration was broken as someone entered the room, the echo of booted feet following.

"If it isn't the unit we thought lost, AF313. How kind of you to rejoin us."

"I'd say nice to see you, but I seem to be visually impaired since my last sojourn at one of your lovely medical facilities."

"Ah yes. A shame we lost that installation. The things they were working on made for fascinating reading. Especially the breakthrough they made on permanently turning off nanotechnology."

"That information was destroyed." Einstein had made sure of it, and transmission logs didn't show any of the information having been sent before he wiped it.

"You might have destroyed the facility, but we have the information."

"You're lying."

A boisterous laugh. "Why would I? Soon, the whole world, make that the universe, will know we've finally found a way to eradicate the mistake we made."

"Why wait? Why not just kill us all now?"

"We intend to, but first we need a weapon to

deliver the anti-nanos. The method used with you, which involved an injection, isn't exactly feasible. I highly doubt you robots will stand still while we prick you."

"My friends will kill you."

"Such brave words from a dying robot. To think, you were once a force to be reckoned with. Now you're just a pitiful, dying shell."

"If I'm so pitiful, why all the security? Even blind and weakened, you fear me." Avion couldn't help the taunt.

His captor laughed. "You think I'm scared of you. You obviously haven't seen yourself. I'd say you're only a few days away from dying. Without the technology, you are no stronger than me. Less even I'd say, given how your body is shutting down. You think you can hurt me? I'd like to see you try. Guards, remove his shackles."

"Sir?"

"Do as I say, soldier. I've nothing to fear from this wreck."

Arrogant prick. But in this case, Avion approved.

The soldiers did as told, and Avion almost sighed with relief as the weight of the chains lifted from him. He didn't let his relief show though, instead keeping his shoulders hunched and his head bowed.

"Well, AF313. Let's see how tough you are."

He didn't have much reserved strength left, but he drew on it now. Live or die.

Forget all his training, forget finesse, freed and yet unable to see, Avion flailed his arms. "Come here, you bastard. I'll kill you."

Laughter rang out as the man in charge and the soldiers with him danced out of reach, easily evading his feeble attempt. Avion lunged in the direction of a voice, and missed, his momentum skewing his balance. He landed on the cold, tiled floor.

Flat on his stomach, he panted and pushed himself to his knees, only to fall victim to a jagged coughing fit.

"How the mighty have fallen," said his captor with an obvious sneer in his tone. "Fear you. I've more to fear from the mindless vacuum my wife uses. Get him off the floor and put him back to bed. I've seen and heard enough. He's of no use to me. Bring in the doctors and start dissecting. Let's see what's happening inside his body."

As a set of hands yanked him to his feet, Avion slumped, hacking even harder. Spittle flew.

"Hey. Get him off me," the soldier yelped. "Damn guy might be contagious."

"No, but I am deadly," Avion muttered as he fired the gun he'd filched from the soldier's holster. Before the body could hit the floor, he turned and fired some more, using perceptions to guide his aim. It wasn't just fictional Jedis who knew how to use their other senses.

In moments, only one breath gasped for mercy, and it wasn't his own.

"How is this possible? You're blind. Your nanos are dead."

"But there's nothing wrong with my ears or skills, asshole. Thanks to the military, I know how to handle pain and defend myself."

He especially knew how to kill. Without mercy. *Bang.*

CHAPTER EIGHTEEN

Despite the joking about going in through the front gates, the real plan consisted of Adam dropping Seth and Anastasia off first at predetermined points outside the military perimeter. Seth would be sneaking into the facility from the rear, placing explosives along his way while Anastasia stowed herself in the trunk of a vehicle heading into the installation.

Not that the driver knew he had a stowaway.

The male, stopped at the red light, found himself understandably distracted by Adam, who pulled up alongside him, revving his super car. The sap never even knew Anastasia had popped his trunk and hopped in. The lax gate guards on duty at the parking lot entry point never bothered to check either, waving in the worker once he flashed his badge for his evening skeleton shift on the factory floor.

Too easy.

Once inside, Anastasia also planned to place bombs on anything that would create pretty fireworks.

Also known as a distraction.

Operating on a scrambled frequency, they sent short encrypted messages to keep each other in the loop so as to perfectly time the assault.

I've placed the last of my explosives. Waiting for countdown to arm the timers remotely.

I've still got one more, Seth replied.

Let me know when you're ready, Adam

answered, fingers drumming his steering wheel. Parked a half-mile from the main gate, his part in the plan involved him actually ramming into the place, guns blazing and drawing even more attention while Seth and Anastasia infiltrated the establishment and made their way to the lower levels.

Once Adam secured their exit by killing anything that moved, he'd join them and rely on an unquantifiable hope that his calculations on the chaos would prove accurate about keeping reinforcements disoriented, thus enabling their retreat.

Done. The bombs are all set.

Excellent. Countdown begins on my mark.

Three. Two. No need to say one. The timers were activated and on a short fuse, too. Adam revved his engine and put his Charger into gear. Time to put those pricey modifications to work.

Foot pressing the gas pedal to the floor, he raced toward the chain link fence, which stretched fourteen feet high and was topped with barbed wire. As he powered toward the gate and its flanking guard booths, a pair of soldiers exited and aimed their rifles at him. He could see their lips moving, *Stop or we'll shoot.*

Go ahead. Bullets couldn't hurt his baby. On the contrary, they pinged off his hood without leaving a dent. Adam couldn't help but laugh, a non-cyborg sound that evolved into a "Yee-fucking-haw!"

Not an expression he'd ever used before but which felt apt for the moment.

The soldiers kept firing. They should have taken the hint and run for cover or better weapons. A grenade launcher for example.

But their feeble human brains chose self-preservation, and they dove to the side. It didn't save them. His mounted machine guns sprayed the area. First rule of survival—never leave an enemy behind. Acts of mercy could cost a life, and given cyborg numbers were small and finite, they couldn't spare any.

At a speed of over eighty miles per hour, he hit the gate, his momentum great enough to tear it from its motorized track with a screech of metal.

And then he was through, his car jolting slightly from the raised spike strips just past the opening, their sharp spires unable to puncture his reinforced wheels.

The ping of more bullets barely registered. Soldiers ran toward him, firing in vain, but that all stopped as the sky suddenly lit. The two-dozen charges Seth and Anastasia had set ignited.

Ka-boom!

Everything shook. Flames leaped into the dark night sky. Smoke billowed in a thick fog that would choke those unequipped for it.

Sirens wailed, but only for a moment. The brilliant lights illuminating the place extinguished. taking with them the awful keening mechanical wail.

Rosalind had kept her side of the deal and shut down the electrical grid. A place like this, though, had other measures in place. The backup generators kicked in not long after, but the damage was done.

Full-on panic had been achieved. The siren returned with its strident warning. Smaller explosions popped, adding to the general mayhem.

People streamed in a stampeding herd out of the buildings, some in soldiers' uniforms, others in blue coveralls, and, mixed in with them, doctors and scientists in white lab coats. Bodies ran in all directions, screaming. Flailing. Ducking every time they heard a boom or gunfire. They provided excellent cover.

Skidding to a stop before the smaller entrance into the facility, which Adam had used less than a day ago to check in for his shift, he exited his car and patted it.

"If I'm favored by the odds that say you have a fifty-three percent chance of still being here intact, then I'll see you again."

A gun in each hand, Adam headed into the factory while wirelessly apprising Seth and Anastasia of his location.

Entering the facility on the north side.

I am already on the third level. Weak resistance thus far. How about you, wifey poo?

Adam could practically hear Anastasia gnash her teeth at the endearment.

Seth, darling, I am going to lobotomize you myself if you call me that again. I am on level four and seeing signs of violence. Judging by the clues, I think our friend, Avion, has managed to rescue himself. I'm going after him.

Good news so far. As for Adam, the guards usually manning the first checkpoint were absent. Probably in the first mob that rushed out when the explosions started. About to head to the elevator shaft so he could drop down and penetrate the lower levels to rejoin his friends, he halted.

Something didn't *feel* right. He spun on his heel and took a peek at the hall leading to the administrative offices.

They weren't part of the plan. The computers in there didn't hold any decent secrets, and there were no cells or prisoners on this floor. Yet…that didn't stop him from walking toward the director's office. Pulled not quite against his will, yet, at the same time, unable to veer his path.

Why am I compelled? Was there a hidden fault in his programming that the military had just now tapped into?

Was he about to walk into a trap?

As he neared the office, a murmur of voices came to him, the sharp bark of the director and the fainter sound of someone replying. It seemed not everyone had evacuated.

However, that wasn't what made the hairs on his nape rise. Nor was it anticipation that he could terminate a man culpable of causing so much harm.

What halted his heart and stole his breath was the feminine reply.

What the hell is Laura doing here?

CHAPTER NINETEEN

How did I end up here?

Laura and Rosalind had been only moments from taking a cab to a farmer's field outside of town where they were supposed to get picked up by their ride, a ride that would take them off planet and out of this galaxy.

They missed their connection. Probably because, as they were slinging bags over their shoulders, readying to leave, the military had busted in and taken them into custody.

Or at least had taken Laura. She wasn't quite sure what happened to Rosalind. Things got kind of chaotic what with all the troops who crashed in, screaming at them to hit the floor with their hands laced over their head.

Given the odds, Laura hastened to comply, but Rosalind, she uttered something in Spanish, lobbed something at the soldiers, which exploded in a cloud of smoke, and, in the turmoil that ensued, disappeared.

Even now that the smoke had cleared, Laura wasn't sure if they'd caught Rosalind or not. Nor did anyone bother to keep her informed. Instead, the soldiers dragged Laura away and took her to an all too-familiar office.

But the director's office didn't seem so friendly and familiar, given for this visit she wore handcuffs and was shoved to her knees before a stern-faced director who, for once, wore his military uniform with all its bars. He was in full-on general mode with a stare so glacial he could have frozen penguins.

For some reason the adage of not staring a predator in its eyes came to mind, and she dropped her gaze. Instead, Laura stared at the shining toes on the director's black leather shoes. In them she could almost see a warped version of herself. How strange because usually without her glasses anything beyond a few inches from her nose turned into a blurry kaleidoscope of color.

"If it isn't the traitorous doctor. Or should I call you cyborg lover?"

She stiffened. How did they know? She and Adam had only recently hooked up. Was there a spy in their midst? That wouldn't bode well for the rescue mission if, in fact, there was even a mission still to speak of.

Did the fact that the safe house had suffered a raid mean that Adam and the others got caught—or killed?

She closed her mind against the thought. He couldn't be dead.

"Nothing to say? Funny, you had plenty to say when you were feeding information to the cyborgs. Did you really think someone with your level of clearance could get away with doing that? They are our enemies."

"Enemy?" She couldn't help a scoffing noise. "They're human."

"Wrong. They're machines. Tools to be used. Or, in this case, discarded since they refused to serve their purpose."

"You're the one who is wrong. They're human. Yes, they have more parts than they were born with. But that doesn't change the facts. They were born human, and even though you experimented on them, their humanity is still there. They're not machines like you'd have us believe. You should be ashamed of yourself. You and all the others who thought that changing people against their wills was acceptable."

"Ashamed of what? We made them better!" The general slammed his hand down on his desk, the loud sound echoing in his office. "Before we touched them, they were pitiful. Many of them dying or infirm. We gave them purpose. We fixed them."

"You made them slaves!" Yelling at the man who held her life in his ruthless hands might not have been the brightest thing she ever did, and yet, Laura couldn't just sit there and listen to his arrogant claim.

"They were soldiers. And soldiers are expected to obey. If some of them die in the course of their duties, then that is the cost of war and peace."

"What you have done has gone beyond that. You genetically modified these men and women, lied to them or outright forced them to become something they never asked for. You took their freedom, and when they refused to be your puppets, you slaughtered them."

"Before they could slaughter us!" he yelled, the spittle flying from his tight lips and his eyes blazing with righteous anger. "We had no choice. Once we realized they would not be controlled, we had to exterminate. So many of them became mad when the programming failed. And mad machines who know how to kill and are virtually indestructible are a threat to the human race. We did what we had to in order to protect mankind."

"How is holding them prisoner here and experimenting on them protecting mankind?" was her sarcastic retort.

"Know thy enemy. Or, even better, discover thy

enemies' weakness and then use it to eradicate them. Did you know we've finally found a way to destroy them once and for all? Just turn off their bots and poof"—he spread his hands in a mini explosion—"they die."

"If you have this method, then why drop a bomb on Adam's house? Why not just poof him, as you say?"

The general scowled as he moved away from her. "Unfortunately, we've had issues replicating the procedure since the original lab got destroyed before they could relay the information. But we're close, very close. Once we discover the secret to turning the nanobots off, the cyborg threat will cease to exist."

One thing didn't make sense. "If your whole purpose is to turn them off, then why have me work on the reanimation of the nanotech?"

A malicious grin spread across his lips. "Because, if we can turn it off, then they no longer pose a danger. We won't need to resort to breaking their minds. We'll just threaten any new cyborgs with flipping off the switch. Once they've been modified, they need the nanos to survive. Just look at your new cyborg friend, AF313. A fragile shell, and once Major Kelly is done questioning him, AF313 will donate his body for the greater good of mankind."

"You're going to kill him!"

"Such shock. He's dying anyway. Why delay the inevitable? At least now he serves a purpose. Unlike you. While the option to reanimate would be handy, it's not necessary in the grand scheme of things, which means you're no longer necessary."

"So why kidnap me then? Why not just have your soldiers kill me when they raided the safe house?"

"For secrets of course. Before you die, I expect you to spill every single thing you know about the cyborgs. Locations. Names. Every little detail."

"I know nothing."

The hard cuff to the side of her head sent her sprawling. She blinked as she rotated her throbbing jaw.

"Let that be your first lesson. Lies will result in punishment."

"And yet the truth will still end up with you killing me? Exactly where's the incentive?"

"Impertinent bitch!" The kick at her ribs caused her to gasp and roll onto her back, arms crossing over her middle.

He crouched down beside her, the coldness in his expression frightening. "And so begins your lesson in humil—"

Whatever he meant to say got cut short as the floor and the very building itself shook, the distant boom of explosions muted, and yet unmistakable.

"What the fuck!" he exclaimed as he got to his feet. The lights flickered and died. Darkness fell, only for a moment before the backup generators kicked in, the emergency floodlight in a corner of his office illuminating the space.

A walkie-talkie on his desk crackled to life. "Sir, computer systems are offline."

"No shit, soldier. What the hell is happening out there?"

But there was no reply. Just dead static.

The general turned his gaze her way. "You knew this was coming, didn't you? We didn't kill Adam and the others in that explosion, did we? That bloody model AF313 lied to us. How many are out there? What's their plan?"

She clamped her lips tight.

He lunged and grabbed a fistful of hair, drawing a sharp cry from her. "Answer me!"

A slap snapped her face to the side. Then another. After a third, he flung her from him.

She put a hand to her burning cheek, waiting for the fear. Waiting for the anxiety that she was about to die. Instead, a focused rage filled her.

Who gave him the right to abuse her? To treat her like this? And why was she taking it?

What else can I do?

The general loosed the top few buttons on his dress shirt and shrugged off his coat before rolling up his sleeves. "How do you feel about pain, Doctor?" he asked as he cracked his knuckles.

"Maybe I should ask you that question, General." The ache in her cheek had faded more quickly than she expected, and she got to her feet to face the man she'd silently hated for months.

"You dare threaten me?" He arched a brow as he laughed.

A surge of adrenaline went through her. Not only did her entire body thrum with energy, but her eyesight had also sharpened, as if the blow had jolted something loose inside her—or moved something into place.

"I do dare because someone has to stand up to bullies." Spine straight, shoulders back, and gaze not wavering, she faced the general. Yes, he might outweigh her, and he might know how to fight, but she wasn't about to sit there and let him hurt her. She'd defend herself to her last breath.

"You'll regret those words," he threatened.

The door to the office crashed open and

bounced off the wall. Adam stood framed in the doorway, eyes practically shooting lasers—which she'd heard those with the robotic orbs could do. She couldn't help but smile at seeing him.

Then screech as the general lunged and grabbed her by the hair, reefing her tight against his chest, a gun pointed at her temple.

"If it isn't the model soldier. I knew we should have killed you two weeks ago when we discovered what you were."

"You're right, you should have," Adam purred in a low tone as he prowled into the office, forcing the general to shuffle his body to keep him within sight. "Why didn't you?"

"The stupid fuckers I work for wanted to see what you were up to. We had undercover squads follow you around to discover what secrets you hid."

"You mean like the fact you had the leader of the Earth's cyborg resistance under your nose for years and never suspected?"

"Leader?" The general adopted a mocking tone. "A pathetic leader of a ragtag group of broken cyborgs and a few measly humans. What was your greatest accomplishment?" The general smirked in evident mockery. "Let's see. You smuggled a few supplies here and there. Rescued the occasional leftover bot who wasn't deemed important enough to destroy. Oh yes, your movement was a great success."

"I made a difference," Adam growled.

"Not really and soon you won't even be a distant memory. In short order, we will have a weapon that will make all cyborgs cease to exist. You will only be a brief footnote in the history of humanity."

"Don't be so sure of that." Adam's gun hand

raised and aimed.

"I wouldn't do that if I were you. Drop it, or I will blow her head off." The bastard pressed the barrel of his gun harder against Laura's temple. She panted, unable to contain her fear. She knew a little about cyborg training. Right now his logical side was telling him to shoot. To hell with civilian casualty.

Yet, indecision froze him. She could see the battle on his face as emotions flitted across. Opening his fingers, he let his weapon fall and hit the floor with a clatter.

Laura could have sobbed at this evidence of his attachment to her, and then screamed because, without his gun, he couldn't defend himself.

The hand gripping her hair shook, but she didn't feel any pain. The general laughed. "Just as I suspected. You do have a soft spot for the human girl. Or should I call it a weakness?"

"Let her go and I'll kill you quickly," Adam offered.

"Or how about I shoot her and then kill you?" The muzzle slid and pressed against the back of her skull.

"You really don't want to do that. If she dies, you'll join her."

"Good point. But you forgot to calculate one thing. I don't need to kill her to best you. So here's a question, cyborg. You obviously care for the girl, but the question is, do you care enough? Will you let her die so you can live?"

The gun at her temple shifted to her shoulder, and while Laura heard the retort as it fired, she didn't immediately grasp what it meant. The pain took a moment to filter. Wet warmth gushed from her. Blood.

My blood.
He shot me.

CHAPTER TWENTY

Adam couldn't believe the bastard shot her. He'd shot Laura, but she wasn't dead. Yet. If he didn't stop the bleeding, though, she wouldn't last more than a few minutes.

What to do? If he attacked the general, she would bleed out. But if Adam stemmed the blood, he left himself vulnerable.

The analytical part of his brain insisted she'd die no matter what he did, but his heart insisted there was only one viable choice.

Dropping to his knees, he ignored the general and the threat he posed to press his hands against the hole in her shoulder, the warm, slippery wetness of her blood frightening against his skin.

Prone beneath him, Laura didn't say a word. She didn't have to. Her eyes, wide with shock, said it all.

He could have sworn he heard her say, *Why? You should have saved yourself.* He knew she said it, and yet her lips never moved.

The cold muzzle of the general's gun pressed against his forehead. Welcome to the end of the line. While Adam could survive many wounds, a direct hit to his central cortex, and his brain computer interface, would signal lights out.

He and Laura would both die here. Unless he removed his hands and hastened her death. The logical part of him insisted he listen to reason. *I can still live.*

He couldn't do it.

The ruthless killing machine couldn't steal what precious moments of life she had left. *I love her too much to let her go.* She saw the choice he made in his eyes, heard it as well, or so it seemed, because she replied in his mind, *I love you too.*

And then his crazy human doctor pushed away from him, with more strength than her fragile frame should have held. She grabbed the general around his ankles, her sudden movement throwing him off balance.

The gun went off, but the general's aim had shifted from Adam's forehead with the motion, and the bullet lodged into the vest Adam wore. Before the bastard could fire again, Adam threw himself at the man, grasping the wrist of the hand wielding the pistol while his free hand palmed a knife and slid it with ease into the heart—if the general even had one—of the man who'd caused so much pain to cyborgs. The man who'd just taken away the one thing Adam cherished in life.

The wound he delivered was a killing blow, one Adam didn't need to watch, not when Laura probably breathed her last. Without his hands stemming the blood, she'd bleed out. Or already had.

He made a noise, half rage, half disbelief when he grabbed at her and realized the wound no longer pumped wetly.

Too late. It was too late. She was gone. Dead. Lost to him. And now he was lost. Alone. He hugged her to him, trying to grab what warmth he could from the dying woman trying to speak her last words.

"Um, Adam, I feel kind of funny."

Already the cold fingers of death came for her. Cradling her in his arms, he hugged her tight. "It's the loss of blood, Doc. I'm so sorry this happened. I never wanted you to get hurt. If anyone should have died, it should have been me. Not you. Never you."

"Are you sure I'm dying?" Her tone emerged uncertain. "Because I don't feel like I'm dying. As a matter of fact, I'm not in any pain at all. Which is weird. I mean the general was smacking me around, and he shot me, and while I do feel a weird tingling going on in my shoulder, I don't feel like I'm breathing my last."

She was also talking an awful lot for someone who'd pumped out so much blood. Adam angled her away from him to take a closer peek at her. No pallor marked her skin. On the contrary, her cheeks were pink, her eyes bright. Odd.

He leaned her farther back to glance at her wound then blinked, not because he needed to in order to maintain his human guise but because he needed to refresh his visual receptors.

"This can't be. It makes no sense." He brushed his fingers across the hole in her shirt, across pale flesh knitted together with only a red mark to show she'd gotten shot. He rubbed at the spot, a spot bereft of blood, almost as if her skin had absorbed it. But only cyborgs absorbed through their skin.

A niggling suspicion made him ask, "Laura, did the general do anything to you? Inject you with something, perhaps?"

"No. Why?" She peeked down at herself but, being unable to see, reached to feel for herself. Then scrambled to her feet with way too much energy for a dying woman. "What's happening? He shot me. I know he did."

"Oh, he did all right." The most terrifying moment of his life. "But the wound is practically gone now. As is the blood on your skin."

Her lips rounded into a shocked O. Her eyes widened as she mused aloud. "It can't be. I mean, I just got a dab of it, and not even in a cut. But what other explanation is there?"

"You're talking in riddles." And for once, he couldn't decipher it.

"That live sample I had. I touched a tiny portion of it with my bare finger."

He took the next logical leap. "The live sample was absorbed by your body and the nanotechnology began replicating." He frowned. "Plausible yet also impossible. You don't have a brain computer interface to govern them, do you?"

"If you mean has anybody been chopping into my brain and inserting microchips, then the answer is no."

"That you know of."

She glared at him. "I'd know. Up until a few days ago, I was one hundred percent human."

"Was. You're something else now, Doc. But we'll have to figure out more on that later. We've still got a rescue mission to finish."

The distant sound of gunfire reached them.

"Let's go find our friends and blow this joint."

And he meant blow.

CHAPTER TWENTY-ONE

Close. So close.

Avion could sense her presence, almost like a pulse vibrating through his body on a mental wave. *I am so damned closed,* but he couldn't move, pinned in place by more guards than he'd yet encountered in this place. He'd only narrowly avoided having his head blown off when his fingers found the edge of the wall and he waved a hand past it.

To those who thought him crazy for attempting to rescue another when he couldn't see and had no nanotech to protect himself, yes, he was nuts. And dying. Huddling and evading danger wouldn't extend his life by much, but he could perform one more meaningful act. More meaningful than just blowing away a few soldiers on his way here.

He still wasn't sure how he'd gotten here, alive. It wasn't as if he hadn't encountered any resistance on his way. But while he couldn't see the enemy coming, he could hear them. As soon as he suspected a threatening presence, he dropped to the ground, splayed much like a corpse. Only to rise and smite those who walked past him.

Lax idiots.

An internal instinct guided his direction. He trusted it even if it made no logical sense. Too many things no longer made any sense. Whatever force steered his steps had led him to where he now hid.

The corner he shielded behind wasn't ideal. He

kept having to split his attention, which, if his nanos functioned, wouldn't have taxed even a small portion of his brain but now took his entire focus. He could only pay attention to one direction at once. How inefficient. He tried to make sure he kept his ears attuned to anyone possibly sneaking up behind him, but given his prize resided within reach, he kept most of his attention on what lay just around the corner.

Judging by the distinct voices, he counted eight soldiers, armed and very aware of his presence. Every time his nose so much as poked out, they began shooting. Luckily, none of the missiles ricocheted, else he might not be contemplating his next move.

How to get into that room? Old him, cyborg him, would have stepped into the open, aimed both weapons, and grinned while he took a few hits as he shot the enemy down.

Broken Avion had to work strategically on less brain power.

It sucked, but he never complained aloud. Once a cyborg, always a cyborg, and cyborgs didn't whine. They got the job done.

Hoping they might have lowered their guard, he eased his face around the corner, his hand tucked just behind the bend, ready to come into play.

Breath held, ears straining, he felt a hot puff of air in his face as he almost came face to face with a creeping soldier.

"Argh!" Ancient cyborg cry. Okay, maybe more a gurgle of shock. Either way, the frantic and sharp adrenaline flooding his body had him moving as fast as his reflexes, his human reflexes, would allow.

Even though Avion was greatly damaged, his skills gave him the extra burst of speed he needed to fire first.

With a grunted exhalation of breath, a body slumped to the floor, and Avion withdrew as bullets sprayed the area. Once the wild melee died down, he heard it. The thump of feet—from behind!

Shit, reinforcements.

Avion spun and aimed, his finger easing off the trigger at the last moment at Seth's announced, "It's us, dude. Don't shoot. The cavalry has arrived. Giddy-yup." The sound of a hand slapping a body part was all too easy for Avion to picture.

"Laura's right. We really don't take anything seriously," Adam remarked. "And just so you know, the cavalry yells charge. Not giddy-up."

"Maybe you clowns don't take this seriously, but I do. We came here to rescue Avion," Anastasia said. "And now that we've found him, we must hurry. While the upper floors are more or less clear, I heard through one of the soldier walkies that more troops are on their way, along with an airstrike team. We need to exit this establishment as soon as possible, or we will get buried in the rubble."

Leave? Not quite yet. "We can't leave. I need to get her first."

"You found the woman you were talking to? She's here?" Seth asked. "But where? All my sensors indicate this is a dead end. Beyond this corner is an empty room with some heat signatures indicating soldiers. Which, on second thought, makes no sense. Why guard an empty room?"

"Are you sure she is nearby?" Anastasia asked. "I also detect nothing, and the schematics of this place show no excavations beyond that space."

"She's here." Avion couldn't explain how he

knew for certain. He just *felt* it.

"Good enough for me." As Seth answered, the distinctive click of him checking his munitions magazine helped Avion tune in to his location. "If my man Avion says she's here, then I believe him. We should check the room, see if there's any hidden passages. Just give me a minute to clear the joint."

"A minute? You take too long," Anastasia retorted.

"Funny, you like it when I do that in the bedroom."

"And as usual, it comes back to sex," Anastasia replied with a forbearing sigh.

"It's what keeps my old parts lubricated," was Seth's snickered reply.

"I can't believe I married you."

"It's true love."

"Or defective programming."

"Entertaining as this is, can we get back to the mission?" Adam inquired.

"One ass kicking coming up," Anastasia announced.

Blind or not, Avion had no problem following the unfolding events. Gunfire erupted, and Seth uttered, almost reverently, "Isn't she perfect? A blend of hot, bitchy, and talented. She drives me nuts, but man, she keeps my circuits buzzing." Such a cute declaration ruined by Seth's yodeled, "I'm coming to protect you, wifey poo."

"Don't make me blow your head off," she yelled back, making herself heard over the gunplay.

"They're both nuts," Adam said, his tone bordering on wonderment.

"No kidding. Oh poor, Avion. You can't see

what they're up to. It's wild. They're doing some weird zigzag thing," Laura explained to Avion, her hand on him guiding him past the corner into the last hall.

He could have told her not to bother. Even without sight, he knew how to get around. Trailing his fingertips along walls and listening, feeling the air currents, using all his other senses. Especially one he'd not relied on before—a sixth one. The human one that not so long ago had been suppressed by his BCI.

However, being able to get around, and in general knowing what surrounded him, wasn't as much fun as hearing Laura recount in absolute awe the way Seth and Anastasia moved.

"Holy Hollywood moves. They're more or less bouncing off the walls and doing somersaults. That's insane. Especially considering they're firing at the same time."

Firing and hitting. It wasn't long before the last gunshot echo faded.

"Nice job," Adam praised from a spot ahead of him.

Despite Laura's guiding touch, Avion leaned into the hallway wall so that he could place his hand along it. His fingers ran across the metallic surface. Smooth. Cold. A ridge.

His fingers bumped over the raised edge of a doorway as he entered a room. A seemingly empty room, or so Adam announced.

"There's nothing here. Just a table and some chairs."

"Don't forget the bodies," Seth added.

"She's close," Avion whispered, the tug in him practically pulsing.

"Or not. Unless she's invisible, I hate to break it

to you, Avion, she's not here."

"She's here." No question. What weren't they *seeing?*

All his focus attuned to his fingers, Avion trailed them along the seamless walls. He went all around the square space until he ended up where he started at the other edge of the door. In between where he began and finished, he encountered nothing. No other doors. No seams. Nothing. Where was she?

She's here. I know she is. It's almost as if I'm right on top of her.

Despite his blindness, Avion looked down. "She's under us," he announced.

They didn't question his certainty.

"Remove the rubber mats," Anastasia ordered. "Let's see if the military isn't hiding something under them."

The rustle and slap of rubberized sheets getting peeled off the floor took the place of conversation. It didn't take long before Seth muttered, "I'll be damned, we found a hatch. And a heavy-duty one, too."

"It's made of lead and some other weird alloy," Anastasia added. "No wonder we couldn't sense it. I wonder what's hiding under there."

She is.

"That's weird. It's got no electronic lock. Just a giant padlock holding closed a hand wheel on the hatch."

Avion could barely restrain his impatience as they snapped the lock then cranked the mechanical wheel. What would they find?

With a creak of metal and air pressure being released, the portal must have popped open because suddenly Avion could *feel* her.

Hello? He sent a mental query, but she didn't reply. Then again, she probably heard the door to her prison open and prepared to meet them.

Oh shit. I'm going to meet her. He doubted she'd be impressed with his broken exterior. It didn't stop his excitement.

Approaching the edge of the opening, Avion found himself halted as Seth put an arm out. "Hold on, dude. You don't want to take a header down that pit. It looks deep, and who knows what's at the bottom?"

"She's in there."

"Let us just peek at the situation first before you jump in the hole. Anyone got a flashlight?"

"A girl never leaves home without one," Anastasia replied. A rustle of canvas and a click.

"What's down there?" Adam asked.

"It's like some kind of cylinder-shaped shaft. A deep one."

"For what?" Laura asked. "I mean, it looks empty so far. Nothing in there at all."

"You missed the far corner," Seth said.

"Hold on to your panties, old man, I'm getting to it. Holy shit, there's someone down there."

Of course there was. Avion had told them.

"How do we reach her?"

"There's some kind of mechanized ladder, but with the power out, we'll need something else. Anastasia, you hiding a rope by any chance in that knapsack of yours?" Adam asked.

"A lady is always prepared," she announced. "But all I've got is modified, control-top panty hose, and it's not long enough to reach."

"Women and their purses," Seth teased. "I'm surprised she hasn't pulled out a tank. I am so disappointed, but at least I packed for the occasion. Multi-purpose rope, my friends."

A rustle of another backpack getting rifled and then the hum of cable being spooled out. Why was it taking so long? All these delays, even if miniscule, just increased Avion's impatience. Did no one understand his need to finally meet the owner of the voice who'd spoken to him?

"Grab hold. We'll pull you out," Adam shouted down the shaft, his words getting swallowed by the dull acoustics in this place.

"She isn't grabbing the rope," observed Seth.

"Maybe she's deaf," replied Anastasia. "I mean, it's possible. Just look at Avion."

"Could be she's scared," said Laura. "Or doesn't speak English."

Or she needed a reason to leave. Without thinking twice, Avion leaned forward until his fingers gripped the cable. He swung himself over the edge and tried not to wince as the metal bit into his palms.

It sucked not having nanos to send a message to toughen the flesh on his fingers and palms. All he possessed was fragile, prone-to-rope-burn human skin. How he'd kill for a pair of gloves, even if his cyborg buddies would mock him for going human soft.

"Where do you think you're going?" Seth said in a perfectly scolding parental tone.

Wasn't it obvious? "To get her."

"Let one of us do it. Come back here."

Where it was safe because he was useless. The broken one. The most expendable one.

It made him the better choice to go. Before anyone could stop him, Avion rappelled down into the prison they kept her in. And that was what it was. A prison to keep her hidden. Contained.

No longer.

"Twenty feet. Ten." Seth counted out the depth left as Avion plunged downward, the temperature cooling and giving him goosebumps. "Five. You can let go now."

With a heavy clomp from his borrowed combat boots, Avion landed on the floor and wobbled. Some hero. But at least he'd kept his promise. He'd found her.

Even without seeing her, he could feel her, sense the energy of her presence, and almost see it like a shining light in the darkness. He smiled in her direction, oddly excited and yet subdued now that he was in her presence.

"You shouldn't be here," she whispered, her voice the softest of sounds. Into his mind ghosted, *but I am glad to see you.*

"I came to save you. Like I promised." *Trust me.*

"Why?" Genuine curiosity in her query.

"Because it's what I do. It's what we all do," he added, gesturing above him to his friends, who surely crowded around the hatch. "We've made it our life mission to save all of our kind. To save other cyborgs in trouble like you."

"You think I am like you?" She said it with a note of incredulity.

His brow wrinkled. "Aren't you a cyborg?"

At his question, a hysterical giggle emerged from her that rose and fell in pitch. The madness in it, thickly bound in sorrow, gripped at him. How he wanted to hug her and hold her, this woman who emanated such loneliness. "Of course I am cyborg. I am the most cyborg of all. And also the least."

The answer made no sense. Not much about

this situation did.

And time wasted.

"Hurry it up," Adam shouted. "We haven't got all fucking day. Round two is coming. This place is ready to blow, and I mean blow."

Avion held up his hand with only one finger pointing, and it wasn't the one that signaled wait a minute. "Ignore my friends. We have a few seconds for introductions. I'm Avion. What's your name?" *Tell me.*

I can't give you what I don't know. "I have no name. Not anymore. They took it from me and renamed me."

"And what are you called now?"

"In here, by them, by everyone, I am simply known as One."

A numerical identification. How familiar. Avion had one too. All cyborgs did. The first thing the military did in their brainwashing program was take away a person's identity and replace it with a meaningless string of letters and numbers. "One isn't a proper name. We'll have to change that, but the choosing of it shall have to wait. It's something that requires thought. Now that we are introduced, what do you say we blow this joint?"

"You mean leave?" How surprised she sounded.

"Yes, leave. Are you ready to face the world?"

But the world is vast. So vast. And the biological ones, they are so many.

I will be there, as will my friends. We will get out of here or die trying. Come with us. Retake your lost freedom.

"Freedom." She uttered the word softly, and he saw the image of a bird, soaring in a bright open blue sky. "Yes, let us find freedom. Let us fly."

CHAPTER TWENTY-TWO

Laura couldn't help but gasp as they reeled Avion from the odd prison in the floor and then forget to breathe as his rescued burden joined them.

Ethereal appearing, the young woman who unwound her arms from Avion's neck seemed outwardly human with her platinum hair, snow-white skin, and slim frame. But one had to only look into her eyes that swirled, the colors and clouds in them much like the celestial storms caught by deep space video, to know she was touched by something not of Earth.

A rumble shook the room.

"I do believe the secondary charges to cover our escape have gone off," Adam announced. "Which means we're a little bit behind schedule. Time to get moving. Rosalind just pinged me and said the rendezvous ship is about to arrive."

"She's alive?" Laura asked as they jogged back the way they'd come through a maze of uniform gray corridors leading to more corridors, most of them doorless. So strange and any other time she'd explore more, but their schedule was too tight, and quite honestly, the longer they stayed, the more likely the military would have a chance to mobilize an offense.

"Rosalind is alive but not happy the military shot down the first ship she arranged to transport us. Lucky for us, a certain ally stuck around."

"Who?" Laura asked.

Seth knew who and laughed. "Aramus didn't

take off? And to think he keeps claiming he doesn't care."

"Oh, he cares. He cares that he wants to be the one to kill you when you finally drive him off the edge," Anastasia replied with a snicker.

Through huffing breaths, Avion, who held the mystery lady's hand while Seth guided him on the other side, said, "It's more likely Aramus heard we were going to destroy some stuff and wanted in on the fun."

"It is fun to destroy things?" The puzzled query emerged from the pale woman.

"It is if it screws with the military's plan to hurt us."

"It is bad to hurt the unmodified beings. It means punishment."

"Only if you get caught," replied Avion. "I would know."

"Less talk, more running," Adam admonished from his position on point. "Keep an eye open for the enemy."

Chastised, the banter stopped, a shame because, while before Laura might have wondered at their levity during battle, now she kind of got it.

Things had gotten serious. Deadly serious. The darkness of what they had to do to survive and save each other could mark a person. The banter and lightness they added between those dark moments helped counter some of the worst of it.

Only inert bodies littered their exit, especially around the doorway to the stairwell, the elevator out of commission due to the power outage. Laura made a face eyeing all the steps leading upward. While an easy jog down, they might prove more challenging on the ascent.

Or would have to the old her.

Laura still hadn't quite come to grips with what was happening to her. She didn't feel any different than before. Felt just as human as ever—and her emotions definitely hadn't turned robot clinical, or cynical—yet there was no doubting she had radically changed. The healing of her wounds, and so quickly, was only part of it. Her eyesight, always a blurry mess without her glasses, now saw things with a sharpness and clarity she'd never achieved, even with lenses.

I can see. And smell on a whole new level, each layer of scent distinctive. Her stamina had seen an increase. Just look at how she took the stairs two at a time and did not run out of breath.

The nanotechnology she'd played with had somehow affected her, so did that make her a cyborg? What defined a cyborg? Was it just the nanos, or did it come from owning a certain metal-to-flesh ratio? She had no ore-based parts. She didn't have a mechanical heart or internal CPU or any other enhancements the usual cyborgs received. Did this mean she could pass through metal scanners?

What am I? The scientist in her was dying to find out.

The fear she should have experienced during the moment of revelation, the hysteria at her possible loss of humanity, and the amount of bloodshed and violence she'd seen in the past few days should have sent her to babble and cry hysterically in a corner. Instead, despite the alien technology running through her blood, she'd never felt stronger and more alive. *I am more than ready to face the world and truly experience life to its fullest.*

Ping!

The stray bullet ricocheted off the metal banister as soldiers suddenly appeared in a cluster above them.

From the top of the stairwell, they leaned over and took aim. Adam positioned himself before her, even as he angled his weapon to achieve a proper sightline.

He and Seth didn't miss. Nor did Anastasia, who counted aloud to Seth's amusement, even as he managed to stay one digit ahead.

The skirmish didn't last long, but it certainly made itself heard and seen. A scream as someone got hit and didn't immediately die. A wide-eyed, startled expression as a body went plunging past the open middle in a quick, if deadly, descent.

In short order, the gunfire ceased, and they were sprinting the rest of the way, except for Avion. The poor man couldn't handle the strain. Out of breath, and hunched over, he didn't protest as Seth slung him over a shoulder and carried him, fireman style, while the woman they'd rescued followed at his heels.

How her alien strangeness drew the eye and begged for answers. Was it wrong that in the midst of a hair-raising escape, Laura compiled a list of questions to ask her, first and foremost being, "Who and what are you?"

Could this frail appearing woman be the origin for the cyborg nanotechnology? Would Laura get a chance to find out?

As they reached the top and the closed door to the first level, Adam held up his hand to slow them.

"We've got company on the other side," he said in a low voice. "Avion, you stay back with Laura and your lady friend. Seth, Anastasia, and I will go first and clear a path. When I give the signal, you follow and you move as fast as you can. Can you run, Avion?"

The blind man nodded. "Just point me in a direction."

"I'll guide him," said Laura.

Before he flung open the door, Adam yanked Laura close and planted a hard kiss on her lips. "I feel an irrational need for luck."

"How about incentive instead?" She pressed her mouth against his and whispered, "Get us out of here and we'll have another shower together. This time I get to use the soap first."

"Hey, wifey poo, can I get the same deal?"

"I will rock your parts, husband, but only if nobody in our group dies," Anastasia replied with a wink and lick of her lips.

"With that kind of prize, I'll even get you fireworks," Seth laughed. "It's win-win for everyone since dying was never part of my plan."

"Pompous idiot. Just for that, I'm going to get more kills than you. We all know I'm the better shot."

"Another challenge? You're on, wifey poo. I am so going to show you who's the man."

And with those crazy words, Seth led the charge with Adam muttering, "I hope I never turn into that old, senile model."

The door swung shut as the trio dove into danger. Gunfire rang out, fast and furious. Sharp cries of pain also echoed, along with shouts for more soldiers. More firepower. And then the most chilling words of all, "Tell them to drop the nuke. They found the girl, and we can't contain them."

Nuke?

"This nuke, it is a bad thing, isn't it? My definitions have it as a nuclear blast that decimates everything in its path."

"We'll die if we don't get out of here, and quick," Laura added. But quick didn't seem in the cards, given the soldiers pinning them down still seemed determined to waste copious amounts of ammo.

"Would you please excuse me? I believe I can help."

The woman placed Avion's hand on Laura's shoulder before boldly stepping to the door.

About to call her back, Laura swallowed her words and watched in disbelief as the portal swung open without her laying a hand on it.

The woman moved into the hall, and the yelling began. "She's here! Oh shit."

"Aim for her head. Kill her. She can't be allowed to escape."

The panic was palpable. Intrigued, Laura couldn't help but edge to the door and peek. Why such fear over a harmless seeming woman?

Blonde hair floating in a halo around her head, the freaky lady they'd rescued walked toward the oncoming gunfire, or what was intended as oncoming gunfire. It just didn't behave the way physics intended.

The woman raised both her hands about chest height, and while Laura couldn't see anything in front of them, the most logical explanation was the bullets hit an almost invisible shield. Actually, more than a shield, it was as if they hit a curved or reflective surface.

Forget an impact, one second the projectiles headed at the woman, and the next, they'd turned around. Turned around and turned into human seeking missiles!

Not one missed.

Gulp.

As the woman calmly paced past Adam, Seth, and his wife, they stopped shooting to gape at her.

"Is she redirecting their bullets?" Seth asked in

awe.

"Yup." Adam's eloquent reply.

"You better not be staring at her ass," was Anastasia's growled reminder.

"I like my eyes too much to set you off, my deliciously jealous wife."

"Not jealous," she grumbled. "Much."

A nudge at Laura's back had her turning to note Avion's intent to leave the relative safety of the stairwell.

"I think it's safe to follow," Avion murmured. "While she is able to deflect close missiles, she won't be able to stop a nuke if it's dropped on us."

"How do you know this?"

"Fucked if I know. I just do."

Then the word nuke hit her. *We have to get out of here before they drop a bomb.*

Snapped out of her shock, Laura scurried after Avion, grabbing at his arm and helping him maneuver the cluttered halls. Blood was slippery, and sticky.

Up ahead, their walking shield kept moving, but no more bullets were fired. On the contrary, the soldiers ahead of them ran for the exit, the same one she'd used for months when she worked here.

To distract herself from the corpses, she focused her mind elsewhere and asked Avion, "The girl we rescued, do you know what she's called?"

"One."

"That's not a name."

"I agree it's not, but it's all she has for now. Don't worry, I plan to change that as soon as we get somewhere safe."

Adam fell in beside Laura and linked one hand through hers as they followed the blonde wonder, her steps so light she almost seemed to float. Perhaps she did. Her bare feet certainly made no sound and left no trace, despite the swirling dust and splatters of blood.

They passed bodies, too many of them, all dead and all human. Laura couldn't help but avert her gaze, knowing deep down inside that they didn't have a choice. *It was them or us*. Yet it didn't make the carnage any easier to view.

Emerging from the building, and surrounded by wailing sirens and flashing lights, they didn't encounter any more soldiers, probably because the last of them had escaped, the red taillights of the Jeeps and trucks vanishing in the distance.

"I parked over—" Adam's extended arm dropped.

Everyone wisely didn't make mention of the smoking remains of his cy-car, or the fact he let out a very un-cyborgish, "Eep!"

Adam cleared his throat. "Shit. That sucks. Especially since I don't see any other intact vehicles. There is no way we're going to make it out of here in time if we don't find some wheels."

"Did someone say they needed a ride?" From the swirling smoke and clouds above them, a voice boomed as if projected through a megaphone.

Peering up, Laura stared as a small craft hovered overhead, the low rumble of its motors barely noticeable over the scream of the air raid horns.

A metal chain ladder dropped from the open doorway in the side of the ship. A face peered over the edge, a rough-hewn one with piercing eyes. He was bald but for a metal patch on one side. The man, a charmer if she'd ever met one, snarled, "Well? Don't just stand there staring. Move your lazy metal asses. I haven't got all fucking day."

"And hello to you, too, best friend," Seth replied just before he grabbed his wife around the waist and tossed her at the dangling ladder. Anastasia clambered up the shaking rungs, followed by Seth at Adam's insistence.

"Don't hello me, you back-stabbing metal bucket. I leave you alone for just a few days and you're blowing shit up left and fucking right, and you didn't think to invite me?"

"Sorry. It was kind of last minute."

Adam placed Laura on the ladder next as he saved himself for last with Avion and his lady.

"If it's any consolation, we could use one last major explosion. That is, if you're up for it," Adam shouted as he aided the woman next to the ladder. She clung to the bars and didn't move, her placid face peering upward then around, as if uncertain.

The smoke hid the human soldier until he stood and fired with a stridently yelled, "Die, you fucking robot!"

"No!" In a romantic move, if a foolish one, Avion threw himself in front of the girl, the bullet hitting him in the upper part of his chest and exiting through his back. Red blossomed as blood flowed. Not a killing blow, yet enough to leave him incapable of climbing. Hell, he would pass out if they didn't stem the flow of blood quickly.

The gunman didn't have time to celebrate his shot, or to fire again. He ignited. A human fireball with no noticeable cause or reason.

Or did the flick the blonde woman made in his direction with her finger count?

"Get up the ladder," Adam yelled as he slung Avion over his shoulder. "We need to go."

This time the freaky lady didn't hesitate. She moved quickly and smoothly up, allowing Adam to climb until he swung onto the flight deck. Seth quickly took Avion from him and placed him on the floor, applying pressure to the injury.

"Someone grab me a med kit. We need to stop the bleeding," he shouted. Anastasia moved quickly to assist him.

"Are you Adam?" the bald man asked. "I'm Aramus. Follow me. We've got some aircraft to avoid."

"So there is a nuke on its way?"

"One? Ha. You all rated two. Just what the fuck are they worried you'll escape with?"

Peering back at Avion, who was watched over by a frowning blonde, Laura had to wonder.

"We might have brought back the answer. But just in case we missed something, and to make sure the military can't use it again, we need to wipe that installation clean."

"This ship doesn't have that kind of firepower," Aramus grumbled as he wedged into a pilot seat at the front of the craft.

Rosalind, sitting co-pilot, didn't spare them a glance, but Laura could have sighed in relief at spotting her.

Adam dropped into the only other spot and buckled the safety harness as his eyes scanned the readouts before him. "I don't suppose your main ship is hiding nearby?"

"Nope. We didn't want her to get noticed, so we tucked in like a baby inside one of the moon's craters. But no worries. Blowing shit up is my specialty. I've got a plan," Aramus announced, his hands flying over his console. "What do you say we have those incoming human pilots blow the joint for us?" Aramus bore an evil grin, which was oddly contagious.

The whole adventure was contagious. As Laura walked on her first ever spaceship—even if just a small planetary explorer one—and entered an honest-to-goodness command center, built for a small crew so she had to hover in the door, the little girl in her who once knew how to get excited wanted to squeal, "Look at all the flashing buttons!"

But it wasn't just the child in her that wanted to push some to see what would happen. She got her chance when Aramus yelled. "Lady with the caught-in-headlights gaze, behind you, the blue button, flick it. Now!"

Such an innocuous looking switch, but as soon as she touched it, they dropped like a stone, and she screamed.

CHAPTER TWENTY-THREE

Adam had just enough time to grab at Laura before she went crashing into a console. "You crazy fucker!" he yelled at Aramus. "What the hell?"

"I need manual control of the ship so we can do this."

'This' involved them rolling and then diving, heading toward the military installation, a nuke hot on their tail.

A good thing his unit wasn't prone to panic else Adam might have worried at the speed with which they approached the solid structure. But he trusted in the skills of his cyborg brother.

Poor Laura, she closed her eyes and squeaked from her position on his lap. He hugged her close and whispered, "Don't worry. He's cyborg. He won't miss."

Indeed he didn't. At the last possible moment, Aramus reefed their vessel into a rising surge. The nuke didn't have time to adjust and follow. It hit the building, and the shockwave radiated out, catching the rocketing spacecraft and sending it spinning.

Adam kept his arms locked around Laura, his own harness keeping him stabilized in his seat. In the back, he could hear Seth cursing. "Bloody hell, Aramus. Did no one ever teach you how to drive?"

The cyborg with the metal skull patch chuckled. "Stupid spy bot never could handle too much spinning."

A red light flashed on the radar screen. "Shit, the other plane launched the other nuke."

And it was right on their tail.

Aramus swerved the vessel, but the nuke followed. "Got any more buildings to blow up?" he asked.

"Not really."

"Any big malls or tall buildings that could use a razing?"

Laura gasped. "What about the civilians?"

"I didn't hear you worrying about that a minute ago."

"The military had it coming. But civilians don't."

"Then what would you like me to do, lady?"

"This nuke thing, it is bad for this vessel?" The woman they'd rescued appeared in the portal, seemingly unaffected by the swerves and dips Aramus engaged in to keep the bomb from connecting.

"Depends on your point of view. Do you mind having your body parts scattered over a few states?" was Aramus' sarcastic reply.

"That would not benefit Avion and the rest of you. I will fix it."

"How the hell do you..." Aramus' query trailed off as the nuke angled away from them, up, up, and away. Even Aramus couldn't help but join Adam and Laura as they craned to peek out the front window of the craft. In the atmosphere, high overhead and far enough away, the nuke exploded in a bright shower of sparks and smoke.

"It is done. Might we now rendezvous with your larger vessel? The one named Seth says Avion needs to go there."

"Um. Yeah. Sure." The ornery male seemed at a loss for words. They all were as the blonde woman moved to the back.

Aramus wasted no time in heading off-planet, hitting the Earth's atmospheric ring, and powering through it before the military forces could regroup and come after them.

Not to say they got off scot-free. A few vessels did manage to intercept, only to get blown to bits by the *SSBiteMe,* which blasted its way out of hiding on the moon, taking out a key communication center when it did.

In short order, the small craft was tucked into the bay, Aramus had rejoined his crew and plotted a course out of the Earth's solar system. Avion rested in critical condition in the medical wing being attended. As for Adam and Laura?

They stood on the command center deck, more useless than an AM receiver on a cyber unit.

"We're alive," Laura said in a wondering tone.

"Of course we are. We cyborgs are hard to kill, especially when given incentive," he replied. "I seem to recall a certain promise of a shower as part of mine."

"You remembered."

"I'm a cyborg. We never forget anything. Especially not something like that." He dropped a kiss on her lips.

"Oh, fuck me. Not another fucking lovey-dovey couple. What the hell is happening to people around here? We're losing our edge," Aramus bellowed.

"And our hearing," quipped a petite woman with a wry smile who perched herself on the armrest of Aramus' command seat.

"Sorry," Aramus rumbled. "But really. This is a spaceship, not the fucking love boat."

"Oh, really? Then perhaps I should find other quarters for the remainder of this trip," said the woman with an arch of a brow.

"Ruined, and by a human woman. It's enough to make me want to find a vat of oil and drown myself in it," he grumbled, and yet, despite his complaint, he still snared the female around the waist and planted a kiss on her lips.

A man seated at a console turned to face them, a humorous tilt on his lips. "I'm Kentry by the way. You guys are more than welcome to go make yourselves comfortable until we figure out our next course of action."

With nothing better to do, Adam, who'd already linked to the computer and downloaded a map of the ship, led the way.

Laura stared with wonderment around her. How strange this must all seem. Even Adam found himself intrigued, given he'd spent all of his cognitive years on Earth. The closest he got to space was a short trip once to the moon for the military as a guard for a shipment.

In the room assigned to them, Adam ignored the utilitarian accommodations—bunk bed cots covered in gray thermal blankets, a small square table bolted to the floor, and a pair of stools—to stare at a screen showing a view of Earth receding.

Laura tucked in close, and he draped an arm around her, hugging her tight. Together they watched the only world they'd ever known shrink. He knew when it hit her. She froze, and forgot to breathe.

"I'm leaving home." She whispered the words.

He didn't sugarcoat the reality. "Not just home but an entire solar system." There went the only way of life she'd known. How would she handle going off into the unknown?

A shiver went through her.

"Are you scared?"

"I should be," she admitted, "but I'm not. More like tingling with anticipation. This is going to sound weird, but I'm free now."

A frown creased his brow. "Free? You always were as a human."

"I wasn't talking about that kind of freedom. More free from a promise to a cyborg. A cyborg long dead. But given all that's happened, meeting you, the others, helping, I no longer feel bound to that promise. I did what I could. I made a difference. What about you? You've been the Earth resistance leader for years. Are you okay with having to leave it behind?"

He'd honestly not thought that far ahead. "We are both free of the commitments we made," Adam murmured as it finally sunk in.

Free to live and love, in the open. No more hiding.

Her thoughts touched him, such a strange sensation, akin and yet not the mind-to-mind speech he and the other cyborgs used. A byproduct of the nanos even now coursing through her body, changing her, but changing her into what? She didn't have a BCI like the cyborgs or machine parts. She was one hundred percent flesh, and yet, at the same time, she was no longer completely human.

"Are you sad we're leaving?"

"A little," he admitted. "A part of me feels guilty that I'm off with the woman I love."

"Do you really love me?"

"After all that has happened, can you doubt it? I might usually only rely on my logic, but where you are concerned, rationality does not enter the equation. I see only one possible cause for that. I love you, Doc."

"It's funny. I once argued with my English

teacher that love at first sight was creative fiction. It couldn't exist, and yet from the first moment I saw you, I knew something was different. It occurs to me that, much like some chemical combinations, it is possible for love to spontaneously erupt. For two elements to meet and bond immediately, and perfectly."

"I couldn't have said it better."

"So where do we go from here?"

"Shower. Bed. Maybe another shower."

She laughed. "That wasn't what I meant. I mean what's next for us? And everyone else?"

"I guess we start over. Set up a new base of operations. Maybe expand our search beyond Earth into the stars. I know there's more cyborgs out there, stranded or enslaved, who need someone to help them."

"Then we'll find them, and we'll rescue them," she said, wrapping her arms around him and laying her head on his chest. "You know I'll help. I also intend to look for answers. The cyborgs need to know where they come from and how to stop the military from shutting them down. I think with our newest member, we might finally be in a position to provide some answers."

"You're talking about that strange woman we rescued. The one with the freaky-ass powers."

"Yes. Did you know she calls herself One? Which is a name we'll truly have to change. I think she holds the key to many secrets."

"Secrets you intend to unravel?"

"Most definitely. But not until later. Right now, I have only one thing I need to find out."

"Oh, and what's that?" he asked, already knowing the answer, as her core temperature rose and the musk of her arousal surrounded him in a pheromone cloud.

"This inquiring mind wants to know how you taste." She shot him a teasing smile, even as her hand slid below his waistline to cup him. The bulge that met her just widened her grin.

"Taste? For scientific reasons of course."

"Oh, yes. And I warn you, this might cause you undue hardship and stress your control, as I intend to be very thorough with my exploration, and experimentation." With those purred words, she dropped to her knees and rubbed her cheek against the fabric covering his shaft.

He leaned against the wall as her nimble fingers worked the zipper and button to his pants. Tugging them down, she almost got a literal eyeful as he sprang forward, his erection more than ready for her sensual promise.

Funny how he could control just about every aspect of his body and actions, except for when Laura touched him. She gripped his cock and stroked it, and he turned into a simple-minded creature. A true human. A man. A man who craved the touch and skin-to-skin pleasure only this woman could bring him.

The fingers she wrapped around him stroked his length, and he couldn't help but groan, "That feels so good." His hips projected forward, thrusting in time to her movement.

"That might feel good, but I bet you I know what will feel better." The tip of her tongue emerged to dab at him. A brief, wet flick. Then a longer, head-stroking swirl. Before he could gasp, she opened her mouth wide and sucked him in.

She truly meant what she said about exploring him and testing his control. Back and forth, she dragged her taut lips, rubbing the engorged skin of his cock. The flat edge of her teeth also teased him, as did her tongue, which did its best to swirl.

Her mouth wasn't the only thing working his arousal. Her hand still gripped tight, stroking in counter motion to her mouth, the offsetting actions tossing him into an erotic turmoil. One he didn't want to end.

She bit the tip of him, and he jerked, his hips thrusting forward. But she didn't seem to mind, as she took him deeper. So deep. Holy fuck.

He couldn't help but twine his fingers in her hair, to keep her there, to guide her, or simply because he needed something to do with his hands, lest they gouge the wall he leaned against.

"You're bloody amazing," he growled.

"I know," she said around her mouthful before sucking harder. *I love you.*

The projected thought acted as a catalyst. Adam cried out as he came, his hot cream jetting into her mouth, giving her the taste she craved.

Before the shudders of his flesh had died, he'd yanked her to her feet and positioned her so she faced the wall, palms flat on it. This was where his cyborg control and stamina truly came into play. Still hard, he slid into her slick channel, the firm thrust drawing a moan of pleasure from her.

"I love you, Doc. I think I have from the first moment you ever pushed those glasses up on your nose."

"Glasses I no longer need," she said between pants as he pistoned into her welcoming, heated flesh.

"Glasses I intend to replace with clear lenses because they're so fucking sexy," he murmured against her ear as his hands reached around her curvy body, one to cup a breast, the other to fondle her clit. As he squeezed the globe and rubbed her nub, he kept thrusting and projecting thoughts to her. Feelings.

I love you.

I need you.

We're going to start a new life together.

Together.

Forever.

The big bang of the universe was nothing compared to the blissful nirvana that exploded between them.

Two hearts, one metal, one not, joined as one.

EPILOGUE

One touched the thick, clear glass with her fingertips. A portal for viewing. How decadent. She pressed her nose to the cold surface and stared out at the vastness of space. So vast.

Free. I am free.

Despite her great mental acuity, she still had a hard time believing it.

A few hours ago, she'd languished in her prison, counting the spaces between milliseconds to kill time, the metal alloys surrounding her muffling her environment.

Then, her prison opened, and *he* was there. The only one to hear her. The one who decided she needed saving.

But who will save him from me?

She didn't allow that doubt to ruin the moment. She allowed him to draw her close, thrilled in the touch of another. She reveled in the freedom he offered.

Freedom at last.

And a chance. A chance to live again—she cast a glance over at Avion, who lay so still on the bed—and perhaps learn to trust again.

She fingered the many tubes and wires leading to Avion.

There is something wrong with him.

I am dying. He touched her mind with a gentleness she didn't know, or remember—but craved.

"Why do you not fix yourself?" she muttered

aloud.

"He can't," said the being known as Seth, who hovered over Avion, fiddling with bags of fluid.

"Why not?"

"He's broken."

Broken? Well, that wouldn't do. Not at all.

But of more pressing concern was what she sensed coming at them from outside this ship. Vessels. Many of them. Armed and intent on destruction. Not all of them human in origin.

It seemed there were those who wanted to curtail their freedom.

And that wouldn't do at all.

The End
Not quite…

Next story in the series, Avion.

Cyborgs: More than Machines series:
- *C791*
- *F814*
- *B785*
- *Aramus*
- *Seth*
- *Adam*
- *Avion*

For more on Eve Langlais and her books, please visit, www.EveLanglais.com

Printed in Great Britain
by Amazon.co.uk, Ltd.,
Marston Gate.